I0451421

Reluctant Alpha

Aaron's Kiss Series Book 7

KATHI S. BARTON

This is a work of fiction. Names, characters, places, and incidents are products of the author's imagination or are used fictitiously and are not to be construed as real. Any resemblance to actual events, locations, organizations, or person, living or dead, is entirely coincidental.

WCP

World Castle Publishing, LLC
Pensacola, Florida

Copyright © Kathi S. Barton 2012
ISBN: 9781938243226
First Edition World Castle Publishing, LLC, May 7, 2012
http://www.worldcastlepublishing.com

Licensing Notes
All rights reserved. No part of this book may be used or reproduced in any manner whatsoever without written permission, except in the case of brief quotations embodied in articles and reviews.

Cover: Karen Fuller
Photos: Shutterstock
Editor: Brieanna Robertson

Chapter One

"I'm sure this is the right street. The man said to go to the fourth building over on this street and then one street up." Diana had written down the instructions just as the man had told her, and Al knew they were perfect. Diana had been her assistant for nearly five years now and knew the woman to be a perfectionist. Al turned where she had indicated, but it didn't seem right. This whole thing didn't seem right. And it hadn't for a couple of days.

They had been in this town for two days now going from tourist place to another having a grand time. But she'd felt like someone was following them since they'd left Munchen three days earlier, but she didn't know why. They were just there on a vacation, a tour of Europe. They were touring six cities throughout several countries and then home again to the States. Right now they were about halfway through the itinerary and in a little town right outside of Jablonec nad Nisou, of the Czech Republic. Her father wanted to visit a chapel there and as it wasn't on the regular tour map, they'd had to rely on the locals to get them there.

"Jacob, see if you can see the street sign over there and tell me what you think it says, I think the translator is in my bag." Al glanced in the rearview mirror to see her father rummage through his ever present knapsack.

"Dad, you don't need the translator to read the street signs, you just have to compare the letters to the ones he wrote out for us. Sheesh, Al, tell him." Jacob had that look again. One that said, "I'm too old for this crap, but I'll go along for the ride." At sixteen, he was a little old for that particular look, but she had been spoiling him since he was ten and he had it down pat. She smiled indulgently. She loved him and spoiling him.

"Dad, he's right. Diana has the street map, and that gentleman back at the pub said that it would be easy to find. Churches that big are not that easy to miss, I wouldn't think." Al's dad, Patrick Bennett, loved old churches and the architecture that was unique to them. He had been a structural engineer until his retirement four years ago, and this vacation was a dream comes true for him, especially since they all had been able to go.

Al was just glad that she could take this time out of her busy schedule and take them all. She had been working harder than she ever had for the past four years and this down time was just what she needed.

Her real name was Alastriona Airic Bennett, but she had been called Al since she was in first grade, even by the teachers. The only people who called her by her full name now were patrons of her art. Al was an artisan, a potter by trade who had become an overnight success when she started using the clay as her canvas. She started out as a true potter, using a kick wheel and raku firing technique that she had learned at her mother's knee. Her mother, a college art professor, had passed away when she was only sixteen and Jacob was ten, leaving a hole in her life that she filled with art. When she found and fell in love with the electric wheel, she started using porcelain, a low fire white clay. She started using it to throw large pieces and firing them to about fourteen hundred degrees in an electric kiln. Having dabbled in oils in college, she started experimenting with glaze recipes and found a whole spectrum of colors to work with. Her genre was nature, anything and everything in nature. The piece that had made her famous was a tree that represented all of the seasons at once, winter, spring, summer, and fall. That piece had been bought by an anonymous buyer that she had never been able to track down.

"Al, look, there it is, straight ahead. Oh my, you're right, it would be verily hard to miss something that large. Quick, Jacob, get my camera for me." Al parked the rental car on the street just in front of the beautiful church and waited until everyone was out before getting out herself. She liked to make sure that there were no bags or purses out so that they didn't become an easy target.

"Dad, it's not necessary to hurry. The church has been there for nearly three hundred years. I don't think it's going anywhere in the next ten minutes." She hugged him to her. Her father and Jacob were everything to her.

"Oh Al, would you just look at those towers, arches, and buttresses. I could spend a whole life time going over each inch of this place. Thank you, my dear heart. I love you very much." He kissed her on her cheek and moved away. She watched him walk toward the building through the little cemetery and then around it, snapping shots as he went.

The hair on the back of her neck stood up again and she looked around sharply. Nothing. Just like in town this morning and late yesterday afternoon. But the feeling of being watched, more like being stalked, wouldn't go away. She knew she suddenly needed to leave, to gather her family and go. Right now they needed to get away.

She moved toward the church in the direction her father had gone when she heard the first scream. She froze; it ripped through her and made her whole body become incased in ice. It was seconds, precious seconds, before her brain could make her feet move. The second scream rent the air and was abruptly cut off. She was running now, slipping and sliding over the wet grass in the graveyard next to the church. Falling down, she landed hard on a stone and it cut into her arm; blood poured from the wound and ran down her arm.

When she rounded the church proper, she stopped. It was if she had entered a nightmare of her own making. She watched in absolute horror as wolves—no, that wasn't right, men dressed as wolves were standing up on two feet and tearing her brother apart, his arm pulled one way his leg another. She knew he was dead because of the way his head flopped around on his neck. Moving only her head, she saw her father. Oh God, her father was lying on the grass and two other men were eating off his stomach. They were eating his stomach, she suddenly realized. Dizziness pulled at her, making her want to drop to the ground and be sick. But she knew that they needed her. She looked for something to attack them with, they needed to stop, and that's when she noticed Diana. She was being dragged away, still screaming and grabbing at whatever she could grab to try and get away from two more. Al started running toward her, not seeing the last man until he bit into her. His teeth sank into her belly and he pulled her down and shook her around like a rag doll. Pain rolled through her; her thought process shut down. When her head connected with one of the gravestones, blackness thankfully took her away.

Chapter Two

"Miss, miss, you need to come with me. Miss, can you hear me?" The voice sounded so far away. Al rolled tighter, oblivious to the pain, keeping her body as small as she possibly could.

"She's in there, but I don't know if she is able to answer us. She might be dead. Poor thing might hope she was." The first voice, a man, didn't sound like the things in the cave with her. This one seemed much younger, his voice less intense.

"Well maybe if you'd back the fuck up and let me in there I could bring her out. And she isn't dead, you jackass, but I'm sure she'll appreciate you thinking she was." This voice was a woman's and she didn't sound all that happy. No, that wasn't it, she sounded pissed. Al decided that she would just ignore them and they'd leave her to die. She wanted to die, needed to be dead. She felt herself fade away again, going to the place she found the most relief.

Al moved back away from the overwhelming light that had penetrated the room a few minutes, or hours, ago. Time had no meaning in here. It was always dark. She didn't like moving; it hurt so much to move. She raised her one good arm up and used it to cover her eyes.

"Hey, you! Come on, lady, I wanna get you out of here before the newspaper idiots show up. If you can see me, just say something, I don't care what." The woman, her voice sounding frustrated, was closer now; Al could practically feel her coming closer to her.

"Fuck off." Her throat hurt. It was either from screaming or from lack of water, more than likely both. It also sounded gravelly and rough to her. Small wonder, she thought. She'd been here for years it felt like.

The laugh brought her back to the woman and her demands to be answered. Had she said something funny? She couldn't remember. But she had said that the newspaper people were coming, Al thought. She didn't want to see anyone. And she certainly didn't want anyone to hear what she'd been through. Wolves, those things were wolves, and they had killed her family.

"Are you Bennett, Alastriona Bennett? If so, I've been hired to find you. The were's that took you are all dead. They won't be bothering you again. I want you to let me come to you so that I can take you out of here, okay?" The woman had a kind of no-nonsense sort of voice and Al figured was used to people listening to her.

"No, I want you to leave me. Please just leave me here. They took everything, my family. I don't want to leave here, ever." Al tried to make herself smaller. That hadn't worked for those things, she didn't know why she was still trying to make it work, but it was all she had.

"I'm really sorry, lady, but I can't do that. Your friend Diana Lake is worried about you. She's in the local hospital being treated for animal bites and exposure. We found her the next day. You've been missing for six days, Miss Bennett. My name is Bailey, and like I said, I've been hired to find you. And now that I have, I can't very well leave you here. Come on, let me pick you up and take you out of here." The woman came close to Al and touched her injured arm.

She tried not to scream. Screaming had sent the things into frenzy, and terror rode through her at the thought of them coming back again. Whimpering and begging her to be left alone, the woman, Bailey, simply picked her up, carried her to the mouth of the cave, and sat her down as if she weighed nothing at all.

"Here's a blanket to cover you up with, might want to pull it over your head. The ambulance is just over there, see it? I'm going to take you straight there and put you into it. Don't talk to anyone. Let them make up their own stories; they will anyway. There will be police following you to the hospital and they'll want to ask you the same questions about forty times before they're done. If you want me to, I can put you into a deep sleep and you won't have to bother with them today. I won't hurt you, I promise. I think you've been hurt enough."

Al nodded and the next thing she knew, she was drifting off into blackness again, not even caring enough to wonder how Bailey had done it.

Chapter Three

When Al woke in a hospital bed, the first thing she noticed was the pain. As soon as she opened her eyes, the entire nightmare of what had happened since they'd gotten out of the car came crashing back like a slow-moving horror movie. The stalker, her father, brother, and Diana, the wolves hurting and killing them, everything in slow-moving pictures. Her screams ripped from her, one right after the other until someone came in and stabbed her with something sharp and she was drifting back into the blackness.

The next time she woke, she used the few seconds between reality and the nightmares to get a good grip on herself and try to control the urge to scream again. She barely managed to hold on, and only moaned this time. She looked around the room, and noticed that she wasn't alone. A woman in a hospital security uniform sat in a chair next to the bed. They stared at each other for several seconds before she spoke to Al.

"Jak se cítíš slečno Můžu ti něco přinést ?" Al knew enough Czech to get her a room and a cab before this had happened, maybe. Now she understood the woman perfectly. She wanted to know if she was all right and if she wanted anything.

"I'm fine, and no thank you. Do you know where Diana Lake is?" She didn't have to wonder if she was speaking correctly to her in her own language. Al just knew that she was speaking to her, and she understood. She was suddenly very scared.

"Ano , ano . slečno Lakeová . Já ji dostanu ." She said that she was going to get Diana. Maybe she wasn't hurt after all; maybe it was a bad dream after all.

While Al waited, she looked around the room again. It was the basic hospital room, she guessed. Pretty wallpaper with floral print. There was, in addition to the chair the guard had been in, a couch. The equipment, with the exception of the IV stand, had been pushed back against the far wall. The television was on, but muted, and closed caption ran across the bottom of the screen. The bed was wider than the ones her mother had been in and the sheets were pink instead of the standard white.

Her body didn't hurt so much anymore. Lifting her arms up to inspect them, she noticed that other than the IV needle still in place on the back of her hand, she didn't have a mark on her. Gingerly running her hand down her waist, she didn't feel any wound there either, not even a bandage. She reached up and touched her mouth and found her lips to be smooth and soft, not broken and dry like they had been in the cave. Shaking now, she pulled the tray across the bed, opened the little drawer beneath it, and flipped up the mirror. Nothing. Not a single bruise.

Several minutes later after the guard had left the room, Diana burst into it, rushed to her bed, and launched herself into her arms. Al had never been so happy to see anyone in her entire life.

"I thought you were dead. We all did. They had to bring in this special tracker to find you. When they found you in that cave, the police actually thought you might already be dead. She said that it would take someone very strong to survive what you had probably gone through. I told her that you were the strongest person I knew and you'd be fine. And you are."

Al looked at Diana and thought she wasn't strong at all and if given half a chance, she'd hire that tracker to take her back to the cave and leave her there. "I wish she had left me there. What about Dad and Jacob? Please tell me that they are all right too. That this whole thing was just a bad dream." She knew that they weren't. She could still see her father's intestines being ripped out and eaten by that…that thing. Jacob…she didn't want to think about the horrors her little brother had endured before he died. But she had little hope that any of it was a dream, or in this case, a nightmare.

"Oh Miss Bennett, they're both dead. I'm so sorry. I thought you knew. They both were killed immediately." Diana looked away from her. She knew something; Al thought she was hiding something from her.

"What is it, Diana? What aren't you telling me? There's something else, isn't there? What is it?" She was ready to run, to run back to where they'd found her and hide. She knew whatever she had to tell her, she wasn't going to like it.

"Those animals, the ones that attacked us, they bit you to the point of almost death. That woman, Bailey, said that they infect people that way, with their bites. They were wolves, you see, werewolves. And now that you've been bitten by them, there's a very good possibility that you might become a werewolf too."

Chapter Four

EIGHTEEN MONTHS LATER—PRESENT DAY

"Ms. Bennett, it's Diana again. Diana Lake. I was wondering if you could please call me? You have that show coming up and I was…hummm…you see, we, that is, I don't know…when you get this message, no matter what…" BEEP. Al hit erase. She had set the answering machine for the minimum amount of time possible for the message part. Al wondered, not for the first time, how long Diana would have gone on stuttering and tripping if she had it set for longer. In the past when it was set to end of call, she had filled the disc. She glanced at the clock over the stove and thought that it couldn't be right. But with a quick look at the microwave, she realized that it was indeed four-forty-five in the morning. She knew it was morning because it was dark outside. She hadn't been that far gone that she'd forgotten it was light at the same time during the day. Sighing, she reached for the phone and then put it back. She didn't remember her number, she thought. Ten minutes later she had the phone in her hand again and the number on the only scrap of paper she could find on the desk. At least she thought there was a desk in there. Wondering where all the time had gone, she dialed her assistant's number.

It rang four times and just when she was hoping she could just leave her a message, damned if Diana didn't answer. Just her luck, she was really hoping to have to leave a short message.

"It's...it's me. You said to call, I'm calling. What's wrong?" Al hadn't spoken to anyone in nearly six months, literally. Her voice was creaky and hoarse from nonuse. She didn't count talking to herself really, because if she did, she'd have to consider that she might actually have gone over the deep end into true insanity.

"Ms. Bennett, thank good..."

Al cut her off. Sighing, she cleared her dry sore throat. She either needed to talk out loud to herself or get a dog. She laughed at that. "Diana, you've worked for me for a long time. We've been through a lot, please stop calling me Ms. Bennett. I'm not that person anymore, I told you. Call me Airic or Ms. Alastriona, I don't care. But Ms. Bennett is dead." She had leaned her head against the cabinet and was slowly banging against it. It didn't hurt, but it kept her from screaming. Again.

"All right, I'll call you Airic then. Your show is in just a little over one week. I haven't heard from you; no one has heard from you actually. Which is quite possibly because your phone had been shut off for nonpayment of bill?" She knew Diana had had to of paid the bill or they wouldn't be talking right now. She had noticed two days ago, or was it two weeks ago, that there hadn't been any messages for a while from her and had picked up the receiver to call her only to discover that there wasn't a dial tone. Bummer, she had thought. Then, not really. She didn't want to talk to anyone.

"And…I'm sure you didn't call to talk to me about the date of the show, or the phone bill. I've been…distracted. And I don't spend a lot of time in the house." Her voice had a tone, one she had heard even in the conversations she had with herself in her head. She looked around the kitchen. Yeah, she thought, I really don't spend a lot of time in the house.

"The gallery owner called and wants to know how many pieces you have for them. I told him I would check with you and get back with him. Are you ready? We promised that it would be twenty pieces and that they would have them delivered day after tomorrow."

"No, I have more." She paused for a long time. She didn't know if this was the right move, but she'd told herself if she didn't get let them go, move them along, they would keep taunting her. "I…I…Diana, would you see if they'd be interested in showing some canvas work of mine too? They're oils? I've been painting, you see. I have the pottery pieces, about…more than we told them and some art too. It's different, a different style, well, the paintings are anyway." Al waited. She knew that Diana would do it, if only because she had asked her to, but she might not be too happy about it.

"Can I see them first?"

She heard the hesitance in her voice. She didn't blame her. Al, or Airic she was calling herself now, had been a lot more than distracted as of late. And they both knew it.

"Yeah, I guess. But they want it soon, don't they? Are you coming here, or do you want me to just send it with the rest of the stuff?" Please say send it; please say send it, went around and around in her head.

"No, I'll come there. I can be there by lunch time. Airic, hummm, when was the last time you…when was the last time you were out of the house?" That hadn't been the question she wanted to ask, but it was good enough to get her point across.

"Same as always, during the last full moon." She hung up. She didn't want to talk about anything, especially that.

Chapter Five

Diana showed up at eleven-thirty. And almost turned around and left again. The house, usually so spotless, was a mess. No, not a mess. She was sure it was just this side of being condemned. Just. She went to the phone and made two calls. One was to a local cleaning service, and yes, ma'am, they could be out within the hour, and was she sure she needed ten cleaners? Yes, she assured them, ten. The second was to the local grocery store. They agreed, especially when she mentioned the bonus if they could be here at six pm, that they could and would deliver food stuffs to this address.

Walking around the house, she spied the mail. It looked as if Ms. Ben—err Airic hadn't opened anything since the last time she'd been there. Well, that explained the phone bill. And when the desk had been too full to handle another piece, she'd simply thrown it in the vicinity of the desk. She started to sit down and take care of it, but decided to go and find her boss first. She figured she was in the studio, and wasn't wrong. Walking out over the field to the back of the property, a good mile from the main house, Diana could hear the pounding music from a good hundred yards away. Apparently, she was working.

She opened the door cautiously and stepped in. The room was pristine. All along the walls were movable shelves, and on each shelf was a piece of pottery, fired, glazed, and ready for shipment. Each piece was packed in bubble wrap first and then a large, wooden framed structure surrounded it. She did a quick mental count and was surprised to count fifty-six crates. Shit, she wasn't kidding, she really had been working. There was another room to her studio, this one that was off limits to most anyone who came by. Diana went to the door and found it unlocked. There was also a note written in paint on an old newspaper. It said, "D, enter at your own risk." She did, opening the door carefully, and was immediately assaulted by the music throbbing out of the speakers all around the room.

Airic had always had music playing when she worked, but this was vastly different. The usual was classical, Mozart, Beethoven, and Bach. This was more hard, hard rock. And very loud. Extremely loud. Frowning, she moved over to the wall just behind the wheel.

She watched her work. Diana had always been in awe watching Airic work the wheel ever since she had started working for her. Airic was centering a lump of the white porcelain by interlocking her hands and pushing down on it with her upper body weight. She was using her hands to force the clay into the shape she wanted. Once it was the way she wanted it, she took a wet sponge from the nearby bucket and using its moisture, she pushed a well in the center and began pulling the sides of the soft clay up with her fingers at the same time. The shape of the piece started out tall, about ten inches with straight sides. Then with another dip of the sponge, she flared out the lip, gently curving it under, guiding it into the shape she wanted. Grabbing a metal tool from the tray in front of her, a tool that she had no doubt made herself, she finished off the piece by putting a "foot" on it, a smooth, rounded edge that cupped the body of the piece to the completed edge. When she completed that, she picked the finished piece up with the bat, a flat square of masonite that had been varnished, and pushed it to the portable shelving unit she had situated next to her wheel within easy reach.

Airic must have caught her in the corner of her eye because she jerked to look at her suddenly, nearly dropping the piece she had just finished.

"I'm sorry, you were working and I didn't want to interrupt you." She had to shout over the music, but it looked as if she had heard her. She watched as she got up and turned the music down but not off.

"I have you ready to go on the pottery and the moving van will be here sometime after two-thirty. If you want to look at any of the pieces, then I'll have to uncrate them. I didn't think about you wanting to see it." She moved to the big stainless steel sink and began washing up. The clay was everywhere, running down her legs and into her shoes. It was also in her hair. But Airic didn't seem to notice it or care about that.

"No, that's all right, I know your work as well as anyone. Hummm, I hope you don't mind, but I set up a cleaning crew to come in and try to find the house. It seems to have gotten a little messy. Also, there will be food delivered at six. I told them to bring you lots of meals that required little to no prep time. I'll have the crew clear out the fridge first thing when they get here. Before I leave, I'll sort through the mail and pay what needs to be done right now. The rest I'll take with me. I'm going to have the mail sent to the office from now on, if you don't care." She had taken out her PDA and was checking off her list as Airic finished cleaning up.

"No, that's fine. I've been distracted, as I said earlier. The house sort of got away from me. I've...I spend a lot of my time out here, not so much in the house unless I'm starving. I was making due with whatever I could find still in the house, or pizzas. I sleep on the cot over there most nights." She had finished up and was leaning against the sink, and Diana thought she looked...nervous, maybe even a little scared. That was so out of character for her that she could only stare.

"Airic, what is it, what's wrong?" She wanted to reach out and touch her, but knew from the past that she didn't want to be touched, not in any way.

"The paintings...there are a lot. I..." She looked over to the wall where an easel was standing and several canvases were stacked against the wall, all of them facing away from the room. "I...they were an outlet, something I had to do. I couldn't work on the regular stuff, the wheel, without...I had to paint in order to throw. The paintings, they're alive to me."

Chapter Six

"Okay, I mean they feel alive, not are alive. That isn't any better, is it?" She didn't know how to explain to her. Diana would surely call the men with the butterfly nets as soon as she left her. Maybe that's just where she needed to be, she thought, in a padded room.

"Why don't you just show them to me?" When she started walking over to them, Airic was actually relieved. Maybe if she saw them then she'd take them away. She turned the music up a little more as she walked by the radio.

It didn't really help, not unless it was really loud. She could hear every little sound now. The wind blowing through the trees if the windows were open, even the leaves tumbling across the yard the other day. It was driving her insane. The other day she had searched for nearly an hour for a sound in the house she was hearing. It turned out to be the neighbor's cat purring on her deck. She chased it off, not very nicely, but it hadn't been back to annoy her since.

The pictures didn't talk to her. That wasn't what she meant when she'd told Diana they felt alive, but she could feel what they were trying to tell her. She was supposed to paint them so that others could see, realize. She watched as Diana turned over the first canvas and held her breath.

"Oh my. Oh my, my, my. Ms. Ben...Airic, they're...they're very powerful, aren't they? I know what you mean. They do look alive. I...it's beautiful, mesmerizing, tragic...I love it. Are there more? Like this one, are there more?" She began flipping over the others; there were perhaps ten or so in the same genre that was still in this part of the building. When she stood back and looked at them, so did Airic. They really were tragic, she thought.

The first one was done with bold colors of deep reds and even deeper blues. It was of a cave, not her cave, but one with stalagmite and stalactites in it. When one looked closer, deeper into the paint, colors, and the painting itself a person could see the wolf. His coat was dark, so dark it was almost indecipherable against the walls of blue. He was changing, shifting, moving from the form of a man into a wolf. The change had started at his hind legs and moved to the face of a man, blurred by the darkness. The others were the same, moving the wolf through the change in different areas of nature, but always just dark enough, blurred enough that one wasn't quite sure if that's what he or she was seeing.

"Your signature, you signed these differently. Why?" Diana had knelt down in front of the fourth painting to look closer at it.

"I don't know. I...it seemed important that they were apart. I don't care if they're together in the show, that people are aware that they're mine, if they'll take them that is, but they needed to be different. I'm different when

I paint them." She was sure she wasn't explaining it correctly, but Diana just nodded again.

"Oh, they'll take them. I've no doubt about that. In fact, I'm betting they sell faster than the pottery pieces, unless they are the same style. But you'd already said that the pottery was the same as before, didn't you? Oh Airic, these are wonderful. Is this all of them?" She didn't turn, so she didn't see Airic flinch.

She almost said yes, yes that's all, but in the end, she showed her the others. There were fifty-six of them as well. For each pottery piece there was a corresponding painting, though not the same style. She'd had to complete a painting or at least start it before she could throw a piece. If she didn't, then the wheel would just turn and she wouldn't be able to center the clay. It was as if there was some force holding her back somehow.

All the paintings were dry enough to cart up but the last six, the oil still damp to the touch. But Diana insisted on taking them all with her too, loading the last ones into her Hummer all in different areas of the car.

The moving van arrived on time and was loaded and ready to roll by the time the cleaning crew had gotten the biggest part of the house finished and was now finishing up in the kitchen. They said that they might not be able to get the laundry finished, but there were clean sheets on the beds and clean towels in all the linen closets.

Airic had been ordering extra things over the Internet, she was ashamed to admit. In fact, if she remembered correctly, she had just ordered another two dozen towels a few days ago. The trouble with doing the laundry, she thought, was it wasn't just a matter of throwing stuff in the washer. You had to gather it and sort the stuff because if you didn't everything was linty the next time you wore it. She'd learned that the hard way; the little fuzzies made her sneeze for a week. Then and only then could it be put in the washer, not too much though. Another hard lesson learned; measure out the liquid stuff and hope nothing the wrong color was now making everything you owned bright pink. Of course, then there was the dryer! *Sheesh,* she thought, that thing was a terror. If you didn't remember to turn the stupid thing on, the clothes soured. Too gross to think about. And it could shrink a shirt to the size a doll could wear in thirty minutes.

Diana put away the food that had arrived promptly at six and stayed long enough to go through the mail and make a hot dinner for them both. Airic had lost a great deal of weight, Diana had pointed out, and fussed at her during dinner because she was picking at her food. She really hadn't thought about actually eating for a while now and rarely had much of an appetite.

Airic had always been plump, overweight actually, but she didn't care. There were curves where there had only been excess fat, muscle where there had been flab. She had had to get out the treadmill a few months ago. The energy burning through her made her jumpy and sore, achy really. Running had helped with that and the extra weight loss as well, she supposed.

"Airic, are you seeing anyone? I mean about the changes. I've sent you the information on the lady who said she'd help you that's local." She had hoped they could get through this without her bringing it up, but it wasn't to be. Airic knew she meant well, she knew that Diana had her best interests at heart, but the she just wanted to be left alone about it.

"No. And I don't need any help. I'm doing just fine on my own. Just fine if you consider that once a month I'll get as hairy as the lady next door's dog. But of course you know that, don't you? All your packets and information you send me, I want you to stop, please. I don't want to go to someone else. I want to die. To be dead, forgotten." Airic hated that she was taking it out on her; all of it had been her fault, not Diana's. But she couldn't seem to stop herself.

"You've lost weight, a lot of it too, or haven't you noticed that either? What is it, about fifty pounds more? And if the dark circles under your eyes are any indication, you're not sleeping worth shit either. I've been in your house Ms. Bennett, and I can see what you've been doing out here too. It won't go away, ever. You were bitten, not killed. You've lost your family, I know that. I can see them as clearly as…I got bit too, you know." Diana stood up and walked to the door to leave, Airic just knew it.

"But do you change every full moon, Diana? Does every single bone in your body break and pop with the pain so intense, so horrible that you pass out from it? Does your skin suddenly grow hair that covers your entire body? Your jaw elongate and fangs tear through your mouth, making you bleed? Do you have to run on four legs, on paws, being careful not to be seen so some fucking farmer doesn't mistake you for an animal and shoot you? No. No, you don't. So don't tell me what you've lost. I lost my life, all I was; all I'll ever be was ripped from me. Because I wanted to show off and take my family on the vacation of a lifetime!" She swiped angrily at the hot tears and turned away from her.

"Airic, I'm sorry, I'm so sorry."

31

When Diana reached to touch her, she moved away from her. She could see the pain in her eyes, the hurt, but she was hurting too. "I'd like for you to go, please. I'll contact you tomorrow. I've had a really bad day and I...I think I'll go take a nap." She walked out of the room and to the stairs. She heard Diana follow her into the hall.

"Don't. Please don't make me leave. I'm sorry. You're right. I've been...I've been a martyr, and a bitch. Please. I'm sorry." Diana laid her hand on the banister and cried.

Airic walked over to her and tentatively pulled her into her arms while she wept. "I'm sorry too. Let's not...I need you to be my friend, not my counselor. I don't have any friends; they're all afraid I'll eat them. I'm sorry, that wasn't funny. I'm kidding." It was the first time anyone had touched her in eighteen months, two weeks, and four days. She wished it had been longer.

Chapter Seven

"I swear to…if you do not stop with the stupid shit I'm going to have David put both your asses in jail. Forever! We'll see how that makes you feel. Every day for the past two weeks I've had to smooth someone's fur because of you two idiots. I've had it! You will clean out the stalls, every fucking one of them, for the next month, every stall, every day for an entire month. Do. Not. Say. A. Word." Bradley was breathing hard and barely keeping his wolf inside. His "get out, now" had the two boys nearly falling over their chairs trying to get out of his office.

When someone knocked on his door several minutes later, he was no closer to calming down than before. "Come in!" He snarled out. He knew it was unreasonably loud, but he was pissed, damn it.

"Is the coast clear? I saw those two young pups running outta here like the hounds of hell were after their butts. Hope you didn't cut them any slack. I certainly didn't cut you any when you did the same thing twenty years ago." His grandfather sank down in the big chair across from Bradley's desk and sat his feet up on it.

Bradley couldn't say anything because that's where his feet were currently at. He just hoped Martha, the housekeeper and cook, or heaven forbid, his grandmother, didn't catch them. The punishment he'd just given those two boys would seem like a walk in the park.

"I did not paint anyone's house bright orange and toilet paper every tree on their property." At least no one had caught them doing it, he thought. He smiled at the memory.

He and David had been about the same age as the two he had just ordered stall duty. David had scoped out the house for over a week, watching to see when they'd be gone and how long they'd have to do their job. Funny how that had been useful in his later career as a cop. Anyway, Bradley had gotten the paint, not orange, but robin's egg blue, because David had said it would draw less attention to them when they bought it, and waited. It had taken them most of the long day to get it done, painting the windows and doors over too. The job had turned out better than they thought. Then they had bathed in the river, washing all of their evidence down the stream. They had been smart, though, unlike these two. David and he had painted the house buck naked, bare-assed, without any clothes to find. Which was how Phil and Daniel had been caught. Their own mother had ratted them out to him, their alpha. The sun burn on Bradley and David's butts had been so worth it. To this day, no one knew for sure who had done it. Grandda had only thought they were guilty, but had never been able to prove it. *Never will, old man,* he thought with a sneer.

"Sure you didn't. What do they have to do, paint the house again? Mow the pack lawn with scissors? Tell me!"

Grandda moved forward in his chair and reached for the whiskey bottle sitting on the corner and a short glass.

"Cleaning stalls, all of them, for a month. If Grams catches you with that, she's gonna have a kitten or two. And if she asks me, you might as well know I won't lie to her." He just stared at him, watching as he poured two fingers of the smooth liquor in the glass, glanced around, and tossed it back in his throat with a small salute and smile. He put the glass on the bottom of the small stack of others.

"She won't know to ask you about it if you don't let on like you know anything. Damn woman is driving me insane with all her healthy living crap. 'You can walk over to the house, it's not so far. And you'll save gas too.' Wouldn't even let me take the golf cart over here. Isn't that what it was bought for? For me to ride around now that I'm in my golden years? What's a man to do, I ask you?" Bradley let him rant. It was an old argument he'd been having with himself for over a month now since Gram had read in some magazine that one was only as young as he or she felt. She apparently felt Grandda needed to feel a lot younger.

The phone rang and he reached over to answer without moving his feet to the floor. If those two had gotten in trouble after leaving his office, he was gonna kill them himself.

Chapter Eight

"Hello, Wolff speaking," he barked into the phone. Okay, that was harsh. Even his grandda raised a bushy eyebrow at him. He didn't even know if it was them and had nearly taken the ear off the person at the other end.

No one said anything for several seconds, so long in fact that Bradley had thought they had hung up. Just as he was about to ask if anyone was there, she spoke up.

"Hummm…I…maybe I should call back some other time, like when you're not around." The female voice didn't sound scared, but humored about his tone.

"Sorry, bad morning. Perhaps I should start over. This is Bradley Wolff, may I help you?" Better, but not quite his usual charming self.

"Hummm, well, okay. You know my boss is like that too, all snarly and snarky. You two should probably meet sometime. This is Diana Lake, we spoke the other day. At least I think it was you. I didn't get a first name, and that guy was considerably…politer. I'm calling about the gallery in the Merchant district and the show this weekend."

Bradley sat up in his chair so quickly that his grandda raised the other brow. "Ms. Lake, yes, this is Bradley. Everything is set here; do you know if the piece count will be what we were promised?" He was so excited about this opening. It was the first visiting artisan for the "Nature's Eye" and his first grand showing with a professional. Then there was the artisan herself.

He had never met Ms. A. A. Bennett, but he had been collecting her art since before she was famous. He actually had two of her vases. He had gotten one at an estate auction a few years ago, and the other he had purchased at her first show in New York.

When his partners had decided to open an art gallery, he wanted to be in charge of it. It wasn't much of a fight as his other partners had wanted nothing to do with it. Kyle had taken over the running of the nightclub and hotel combo called the Blood Moon, Aaron had taken the casino, the Golden Glory, and Colin had wanted the grocery stores, both of them. Their company, B.A.C.K. inc., had been doing very well since they had practically purchased an entire city and made it their own little slice of nonhuman heaven. It was mostly run by the vampires and wolves in the combined areas, but there were a few humans mixed in as well.

"About that, I have great news for you. She actually has had a very good couple of months, so I have more than we agreed upon. And some art, oils on canvas, if you're interested. Canvases she called them. This is new for her, and if you're not interested, which I believe would be a major mistake, then I'll simply put them in another gallery. This isn't a pressure sell, Mr. Wolff, but I've never...these pieces are amazing. I've...I can't tell you how…you must see them before you decide, of course." He could hear her excitement and her awe.

"I would, like to see them, I mean. When can we get together? The showing is in eight days, so if we need to make changes to the rooms, then we will need to get them into the gallery as soon as we can." He had never met this woman either and pictured her as a small tornado.

"I'm actually driving into the city now…would you hang on a second?" He had heard another voice shriek in the car, but nothing more than that as Ms. Lake had obviously muted the phone from him.

"Mr. Wolff, I have…Ms. Bennett is here with me and I need to drop her off first. She had quite a few errands to run, it seems. But I can meet you in front of the gallery in say…twenty minutes. The truck has already arrived, I understand, and they are unloading the pottery pieces now. Most of the canvases are with the pottery. I have an additional six with me now that are still wet. Would that be acceptable to you?"

"Of course, twenty minutes. I'll see you there." Bradley hung up the phone and stood.

"Where you headed? Can I come?"

Bradley didn't really want to take his grandda, but he had little choice it seemed as he was putting on his coat as he asked. "I'm going to the gallery. I suppose you can come if you can behave yourself. No flirting, and keep your paws to yourself. I'm trying to make a good impression, all right? And as much as I love you, Grandda, I will tell on you about the whiskey if you give me any problems." Bradley knew it was useless to say these things to him and they both knew the threat was empty, but later, if he had to kill him, it would be as good a defense as any other.

"See how you are. You're just jealous because I get more ladies than you do. Maybe you and I should go to the Blood Moon together, leave your grandmother at home. I could show you a few moves that will get you laid if you want."

Bradley just looked at him with an open mouth. His grandfather had not just said that to him. "You know, I might have to kill you here before we leave instead of doing it when we get back. Have you any idea what it means to behave at all? I am not going to the Blood Moon with you and if I even hear of you going there without Grams, I swear to you I will…I don't know what I'll do to you, but it won't be pleasant for you." They had made it to the car and he was delivering his threats to the now closed door on the passenger side. Bradley leaned his head against the roof and banged it slowly and repeated over and over to himself, *I will not be like him when I'm old, I will not be like him when I'm old.* He raised his head up when he heard the window crank down.

"Hey! Pup, we going, or are you gonna nap on your car instead?"

Yeah, I will not be like him when I'm old.

Chapter Nine

"I don't know why you think I need to wear a dress to this stupid thing. I have worn pants all my life and no one cared one whit about it." She had bought a dress over the Internet. Not a smart move in the first place because she had bought the size she had been wearing pre-accident. Airic didn't even realize she'd lost any weight until Diana had pointed it out. The second was she had stupidly bought one that was puce. Who the hell wore puce? But in her defense, the description had said mauve.

"You said you'd go, and you'll wear a dress because it's the professional way to do it. I can't keep telling people that you're sick all the time. Do you want them to think you are sickly and not a reliable person? And you are going shopping with me because you have absolutely no taste in clothes. Just look how you're dressed. Jogging pants and a sweatshirt are all right in the studio, but out in public, it's a no-no." Diana made that noise in her throat again, the one she made every time she was trying to make a point. It sounded snarky to her, but she wasn't sure.

"I do not have bad taste in clothes. You liked that thingy I got yesterday." Airic was getting more nervous the closer they got to the boutique. She didn't want to admit that she was wearing these clothes, not as a fashion statement, but because the pants had a string in them and she could keep them up around her butt. Underwear didn't have ties, but she had fixed that problem with a safety pin. The sweatshirt was a necessity because her bras were all way, way too big and she felt as if she'd be "flopping" around and she didn't want to subject people to that poor sight.

"Airic! That was pajamas! That so does not count as clothes. This lady, Elaina Spencer, is supposed to be the place to shop for these things. She does all the beading by hand." Diana consulted the map again.

"Beading! You didn't say anything about beading. I'm going to be sick. Pull over, please; I need to throw up again." Diana ignored her like she had the last three times she had claimed to be sick and wanted to throw up. "Isn't there some written rule somewhere that you're supposed to kiss my ass and suck up or something because I sign your paychecks? I could have sworn I saw that somewhere in the 'How to be a Great Employee' handbook somewhere."

"Well, I've had it updated and it now says that if you want to keep said great employee, you kiss her ass and suck up. Besides, I sign your name better than you do. You'll love this shop. I talked with that guy Bradley Wolff's assistant and she said that she does all the clothes when there is a big to-do."

She felt Diana look over at her again. She felt like one of those lab projects where a person had to keep an eye on it or it would blow up or something. She didn't say anything for a few minutes. She didn't want to shop, had hated it even before. But this was different; she was going to have to go to her own opening, something she hadn't done since the very first one. And she was going to have to wear clothes she knew she wouldn't be comfortable in, and she knew Diana would insist that she wear heels too. Beading, for goodness sake. Who wore beaded clothes?

"You didn't get to show him the paintings then?" Diana had mentioned that she hadn't been able to see Bradley Wolff, the gallery owner, and then when she mentioned shopping, it pushed the fact that she had left her paintings with a stranger.

"No, he called the gallery and told them that he wasn't going to make it even before I got there. Mallory, his assistant, said that he was sorry, but he'd had a minor fender bender and his car wouldn't be serviceable until later. So, he's going to look them over, including the wet ones, and call me at your house tonight. Are you mad because I left them?"

Actually, she was, but done was done. "No, I'm not mad. I mean, I shouldn't be, right? I just...they've never..." She looked out the window of the car. She didn't know what she meant or anything right now.

"He'll take good care of them, Airic, I swear. I even had them sign a receipt for them."

Airic didn't say anything. She was too touchy lately and she knew it. *Nerves,* she thought, *that was all, just nerves.* She'd get over it soon.

They pulled up in front of the beautiful mansion and got out of the car. Elaine's was painted on the sign in the front yard. There were flowers and rose bushes everywhere. And on the wraparound porch were rocking chairs, several of them, as a matter of fact. And in two of them were two kids, young boys. They looked to be trouble.

"Hey, pretty ladies! How's it goin'? Need any help in the changing room, I'll be more than glad to offer my assistances."

Yep, trouble all right. Airic was all for leaving, but Diana plowed straight ahead, ignoring them as best she could. When they got to the steps leading up to the shop, the bigger one stepped in front of Airic and sniffed her.

"What the fuck do you think you're doing?" It was out of her mouth before she knew it.

"Well lookee here, I found myself a she-bitch."

Airic made to move past him, but he grabbed her arm and jerked her hard to him. The other boy had already trapped Diana against the wall. It was over in a matter of seconds.

Chapter Ten

At first she was scared, then she saw her friend struggling, and suddenly, she was very…calm. There was no way she was going to let her be hurt again. "You'll let her go, now." She didn't even bother with asking or pleading with them. She didn't think it would do any good anyway. She just wanted them to let her go.

"Oh, and who's gonna stop us? You? I don't think so. I'm gonna play with you, then my brother Phil is gonna have his turn." He laughed, turned back to Airic, grabbed her breast, and pinched her hard.

Airic growled. The growl was low, coming from deep within her, deeper than she'd ever felt before. She grabbed his throat with her clawed right hand and lifted him six inches off the ground. She didn't take the time to analyze what had happened to her hand, but gripped him harder around the neck, nicking him slightly.

"You'll back the fuck up or I'll make sure your own mother won't recognize you when I'm finished. Let her go. Now! You should have more respect for your betters, boy." She noticed also that her voice had become deeper, harder than she'd ever heard before. The younger boy must have too, because Phil dropped to the floor and curled into a ball. But her tormentor was trapped; she had him still clutched in her hand. With a slight shake, she dropped him and he too fell to the floor, curling into a tighter ball than his brother had. Okay, she liked this subservient thing. "If you come near me or my friend again, or for that matter, you ever treat another woman like you just did the two of us, I will hunt you down and make you wish you'd never been born. Do I make myself perfectly understood?"

"Yes, ma'am. Never. We shouldn't have touched you. We wouldn't have if we'd have known who you were. Please, we're sorry. Don't tell Alpha; it'll never happen again. I swear." The older one was begging now, and he was stroking her leg with his neck. She didn't know why, but that seemed the correct response to her.

"Go home, and thank your mother for you even being alive. And this alpha person, I won't tell him, because I expect you to. And you'd better believe I'll find out if you don't. Now, get." She backed away from them. The one called Phil crawled over to Diana and stroked her leg too before he stood, still bowed at the waist, and took off running, his friend and brother with him.

Diana just stared at her, her mouth opened and eyes wide. Airic glanced to her right and saw that two of the girls from the shop had come out at some point and were staring at her too.

"What? They were hurting you. Was I supposed to just stand there and let them? Not again." She didn't understand why they were so aghast. Okay, she thought, my hand did do that whole claw thingy, but that happens once a month anyway doesn't it? Maybe it has something else to do with the accident. She mentally shrugged and walked into the shop.

***

"Hello, Mallory, did the shipment arrive?" Bradley was removing his jacket as he walked to the storage room. His day hadn't gotten any better since this morning. But he did have a nice new car.

His grandda had talked him into buying a Mustang Shelby GT500 series right off the lot. It was every man's wet dream and Holy Grail rolled into one, he'd said. He was going to have to have a serious talk with him, he thought again. This car was loaded with every imaginable gadget known to the car industry. The black chameleon paint was a custom job for a buyer that had decided after it was finished that he didn't want or he couldn't afford the car. Heated leather seats, leather-wrapped steering wheel, six speed convertible, V8 engine with 550 hp engine and 19-in. painted machined-aluminum wheels. *Oh yeah,* he thought, *very nice car.*

"Yeah. Couple of hours ago, it's all in the back. Nice wheels by the way." He glanced out the front window and smiled.

His grandda had been driving when that deer had jumped out in front of them, thank God. At the gas station just outside of town, he had been talking to a pack member about a small issue he was having and Grandda had gotten hot. So he slipped into the driver's seat and turned on the air. Bradley, distracted, let him drive them the rest of the way into Merchant area. Had it been him, they might have been really hurt. As it was, his sedate driving over Bradley's pedal to the floor approach had made what could have been a major accident into just what it was, a fender bender, driving into the ditch instead of over the small hill where they had been headed.

"Yeah, thanks. The other one was really old and Danny said that getting parts for it would be expensive. Grandda talked me into this one." He began his trek to the storage area again.

The pottery crates had already been opened, having had a few of the younger pack members come in and do that right away. He looked over each piece and noticed a slight difference to the style. Nothing major really, but she was using deeper, richer colors and the scenes were getting more detailed, more colors too. He supposed that came with experience. He really liked them. He marked twenty for the sales floor and the other thirty-two for the show. He decided to buy the other four for his own collection. He had asked Mallory not to open the paintings, as he had wanted to see them first. He had three opened and sitting against the wall when Grandda walked in the back room.

"Christ! Where did you get those?" He walked closer and knelt down for a better look. He watched as he stroked his finger down the delicate brush stroke along the wolf's back.

"They're part of the show this weekend. The artist that I was suppose to meet here today, well, her assistant anyway. She brought them by for me to look at. I'm supposed to decide if I'd like to put them with the ceramic pieces. What do you think, do you like them?" Bradley moved over to open the next line of six. He liked them; they were powerful and moving. In the three that he had just opened, he felt that she had captured the true shift of the wolf. The colors were dark and almost sinister-looking, but hard and compelling too. He turned to look at his grandda. He was holding one that had been separated from the others and wasn't wrapped. It must be one of the wet ones she'd told him about.

"Grandda?" He suddenly noticed that he was pale. Bradley also noticed that the canvas was trembling in his grasp. He moved over to his side, grabbing his desk chair for him as he went. Shoving it under him, he made to take the picture from him when he looked at it himself. "Holy hell." Bradley felt his knees tremble and he sat down on the floor beside the chair. *No,* he thought, *this can't be right.* No one knew, no one but him and David. It was a painting of David and him naked, painting the Morgan house robin's egg blue.

Chapter Eleven

"Is this it, how you two did it?" Bradley realized that Grandda hadn't been shaken so much as startled and the trembling was him laughing.

"Yes. How did it get here? Is this a joke? David! He did this. I'm gonna kill him." He stood and took out his cell phone to call him. Just then, the door flew open and Tweedle-dee and Tweedle-dum walked in. "Oh hell no. I'm gonna kill you both."

"Alpha, forgive us. Don't let her…please, we're sorry. Never. I swear to you, never will we do it again. We would never have touched her if we'd known. Please, Alpha, tell her, tell her please that we told you." Daniel was sobbing.

"He touched her, I didn't. I even told him that we shouldn't do it, that you'd rip our ears off, but oh no…the other woman, I…she said not anyone, but he touched her." Phil reached over and hit his brother.

"I didn't know. But I swear to you, I will never do it again. Never ever, ever, Alpha, we won't. We already told our mom, just what she said…"

"I told her first, you ass. He was too chicken, afraid Dad would make fun of him. I told her we were grateful for her and that…"

"Enough!" Bradley roared. Both boys dropped to the floor again and curled into tight balls. He knew what they were doing; it was just a reaction to his command, but it startled him all the same.

He didn't use that tone often and not much in the past several years. It was what set him apart from other males in the pack, the ability to command with his voice.

His grandda stood then, taking the picture with him to the door. He sat the canvas aside, backwards to the room, and assured Mallory that everything was all right, that yes, she could go ahead and lock up, and it was after six anyway. He thumbed the lock on the doors to the room and leaned against it.

"What did you two do now? And if you lie to me, you will never see the light of day again." He sat in the now vacant desk chair. He didn't want to have to kill them, really he didn't. He liked their parents, they were a nice couple. Their dad was a good man and had his own limo service that Bradley used on occasion. Such a waste if he did end up killing them both, he mused to himself.

"Just don't tell the alpha bitch, please, sir. Please?" Phil didn't even raise his head, neither boy did.

Bradley shot a look to the older man with a raised brow. "You pissed off an alpha bitch? When, today? You fucking left my office and drove to another territory and pissed off someone else's alpha? Are you fucking nuts? Do you both have a death wish or something? Because if that's all you want is to be dead, I guarantee that's a perfect way to go about it." He was up pacing now and gesturing wildly. What the fuck was wrong with these two?

"We didn't leave the pack area. We saw her at Elaine's on Prospect Street. She was going in when we…" He stopped when Daniel hit him in the head.

"She was here, in our town? Holy shit, you are both dead. Dead, do you hear me? She comes to go shopping in our town and we insult her! I can't help you boys. You've screwed yourselves royal now. I hope you have nice wills made out, because you're gonna need them." *I have to find her alpha and see if I can fix this before we have a bloodbath,* he thought. Her alpha will kill them and will be completely justified in doing so. One did not touch another wolf's mate, especially a female alpha. She would have been completely in her rights to kill them both without a second's hesitation. As much as he'd had to fix things for them over the past few days, he was surprised that she hadn't.

"She weren't mated. That's why we hit on her. She was fresh, you know. A virgin. We could smell her as soon as she got outta the car that she didn't have a mate," Daniel confessed.

Bradley sat down hard. He had an unmated alpha female in his territory. Lynne. Another Lynne was back and trying to take his pack, kill him and take what was his. He was dizzy, he realized; the room was spinning. Leaning forward, he put his head in his hands and waited for the room to slow.

He barely heard his grandda escort the boys out with a stern lecture and a promise from them that they would go straight to their home and stay there until Bradley contacted them. And if they even thought of getting into trouble between here and there, well, he couldn't be responsible for holding the alpha back even if he was his grandson.

"Come on, son, let me drive you home." He felt him tug on his arm and he stood up. He was out to the car before he realized it, going through the motions like a robot. He watched without really seeing Grandda lock the front door to the gallery as he sat in the passenger seat of his new car. Then when he slid under the steering wheel, Bradley spoke.

"Grandda. What do I do now? Am I such a poor leader that even a female thinks she can come in and take my territory?" He jerked back when his head was suddenly forced forward and slammed against the dashboard hard enough to see stars for a few seconds.

"I hear you say something like that again and I will paddle your ass but good, you hear me? You have the word of two idiots who say she was unmated. Virgin! Ha, how the hell could they tell that, I ask you? And you, you stupid fool, what makes you think she wants your territory? Could be she was just shopping and those dumb asses pissed her off. Like they haven't done that to damn near every female in the pack lately. What, she can't defend herself in your territory because you're the wonderful and infallible Bradley Wolff? Grow up." He turned to start the car, and then looked back at him. "Where the fuck is the key hole?"

Chapter Twelve

"I don't like this. I really, really don't. What if I throw up on someone, on someone important? And this dress, what was I thinking? Please, John, take me back to the hotel. I'm not going." Airic was babbling. Anyone within ten feet of her could tell she was either nervous, which she was, or she was nuts, which she was also.

"We are not going back to the hotel. You won't throw up on anyone. You didn't eat enough to make that possible, and you look lovely. Beautiful, as a matter of fact." Diana had said the same thing to her at least eighty times since they'd left the hotel forty minutes ago.

She had fallen in love with the dress as soon as she saw it. It looked like a plain black silk dress while it was on the hanger. But it wasn't, not really. When she'd tried it on, a size three believe it or not, she stood under the lighting of the five-way mirrors and saw the black beading. They sparkled and twinkled, and when she moved, it seemed to slide across her body like a silken hand stroking her. The skirt of it was very short, just a few inches below her butt. The bodice was high in the front, covering her breasts and encircling her neck with a choker like collar. The back was amazing; it hung open all the way down to the dimples of her ass, barely covering the curve of her breast at her sides. Her arms and shoulders were completely bare. And there was a small black bow at the bottom of her spine. Elaine had insisted that she wear a string of black pearls backwards so that it hung down the back rather than the front. The effect was perfect, drawing attention to her long, slim spine. Her thigh-high black hose had a seam that had taken her an hour to straighten, and her high heels made her three inches taller than her five-foot-seven frame.

"Diana, please let me go back and at least change. This isn't me. I can't wear something like this." She leaned over to whisper to her.

"Nonsense. You went from a size twenty-two to a size three in two years, Airic, so of course you feel as though this isn't you. But trust me, you look great! Besides, we're already here." The door opened and before she knew it, she was handed out of the limo by John and was walking in the front door of Nature's Eye.

"Hello, Ms. Lake, Mr. Wolff said to tell you he is running slightly behind, that I was to make sure everything is all right and to make you as comfortable as possible." The young woman that met them at the door, Diana explained, was Mallory, the woman who oversaw the gallery on a daily basis for Bradley Wolff.

"They don't know who I am, right? You didn't tell them I was coming," she asked as soon as they were out of earshot of the assistant. Airic had agreed to come on the basis that no one knew who she was or that she was the artist in house. She had told Diana that she would be able to mingle with the people and get a better idea of what they really thought if they thought they were talking to just another patron of the arts. Really, she just wanted to hide in a dark corner and be left alone. As Airic's picture had never been published, it was easy enough to hide just who she was.

"No. Although, I know there are a few who would give their right nut to meet you. I kept it quiet to both the press and Mr. Wolff and I promise that I'm only going to call you Airic. No one will be able to associate your name with the artist Alastriona Bennett, I swear." She had signed all of the canvases simply "AA," but she wasn't really concerned with them as she didn't really think anyone would look at them anyway. She was just glad they were gone from her studio. Besides, they wouldn't sell, so it didn't matter.

"I don't care which nut they offer you, I'm just glad that you declined." She glanced at Diana when she giggled. Airic didn't think she'd ever heard her do that before. Strange.

They had been walking around about an hour looking at the set up when a group of people walked in. They were quite possibly the most beautiful people she'd ever seen. There were four women and five men. She could tell how they were paired off because the men with their female counterparts kept touching them, running fingers up their bare arms, leaning into them. The single man kept glancing around the room. His date, she thought, he's looking for his date. She turned her back to them and started walking toward the back part of the showroom.

Her thoughts went back to the man as she walked away. She'd like to paint him someday, she mused. He would be a difficult subject to do, his hair as many shade of colors as were on her palate, reds, golds and browns. His body was large and muscular, very wide at the shoulders, his waist thin and belly flat. His hips flared out and were supported by muscled thighs and long legs that she could see beneath the fit of his dark dress pants. She could tell that he was used to wearing a tie; he hadn't tugged at it once like the blond man next to him. Probably a corporate big wig, she thought with a snort.

She'd just gone into the room and was beginning another round when someone grabbed her by the arm and began dragging her toward the back of the building. It was him, the single man, and she was so surprised by that that he had her inside the office with the door closed before she could react.

"What the hell do you think you're doing dragging me around like...like...I don't know what, but I want you to open that door." She moved toward the door and hearing the lock engage, stopped her in her tracks.

"I'd like a word with you, Bitch. I want to know what the fuck you are doing in my territory as an unmated female, and just what right did you have to manhandle my wolves the day before yesterday?" he snarled at her.

Chapter Thirteen

"What are you talking about? Wolves, what wolves? You're insane. Open that door this instant before I scream the place down." He watched her stride forward and he countered her move out the door. She was going to listen even if he had to tie her down to do it.

"My wolves. They were on the porch at Elaine's yesterday and you picked one up by the neck and tossed him to the ground like you're their master. You cut him, was that necessary? I'm the master around here, not you. They aren't very bright, but this is not your domain and I do not appreciate you thinking you can come in here and be alpha bitch and order them around." He knew he was not handling this well. He had talked to both boys and they both confessed to starting the confrontation with her. They had even gone so far as to admit that one of them had grabbed her breast and twisted it. But when he looked up and saw her turn her back on him, he saw red. She was not going to dismiss him like he was some callous pup.

"Wolves? They were your wolves? Then you're their..." He barely noticed that she had paled, that her voice had gone faint. He was too angry to see beyond this moment, this second.

"I'm the alpha around here. The king wolf of this territory. And you'd do well to remember that, Ms…" He turned when someone knocked on the door. Before he could snarl for them to go away, the girl was at the door and fumbling with the lock. "I'm not finished yet. I…" She bolted out the door as soon as the lock opened and was gone before he could finish, heels clicking rapidly across the hardwood floor.

"Airic?" The young woman who stood in the open doorway started after her. He moved to intercept her and was shoved against the wall by the little thing standing there.

"I'm busy right now, but if you'll find…" She slapped him hard across the face. Startled, he nearly snarled at her too.

"What did you do to her? What the fuck did you do? Do you know how fucking hard I had to work to get her to come here tonight, how long I've worked to make this happen for her? And in ten minutes, no, less than ten, you scared her so badly that…oh, fuck you. Where is the owner? I'm going to report you. What is it with this fucking town and its males going around handling women as if they're playthings rather than people?"

Bradley looked down at her and knew with all certainty that he had just did something he would regret for many, many years to come. "I'm Bradley Wolff, and you, I assume, are Diana Lake. And that woman…who is she?" He knew the answer as surely as he knew his own name.

"Wolff, the owner, I presume? Well, that, Mr. Wolff, was Airic, otherwise known as Alastriona Bennett. You just insulted your artist and her assistant. Now, you want to tell me what kind of damage I'm going to have to clean up?" She folded her arm across her chest, glared at him, and tapped her foot. He felt three inches tall.

"Maybe you should come into my office. I grovel better without witnesses." He moved back away from the door and waited for her to enter. When she did, he noticed that everyone in the gallery had already witnessed his dressing down, and Aaron, his best friend and master vampire of this realm, was hanging onto his mate Sara. They were laughing their asses off.

**

Airic ran out into the night, not stopping when she heard Diana call for her when she opened the office door. Moving through the parking lot, she didn't see anything, hear anything. Wolves, wolves, wolves kept circling round and round in her head. He touched her arm before she saw John standing in front of her, and she screamed.

"Are you all right, Ms. Bennett? I won't hurt you. You look like you've seen a ghost. Here, come sit down in the car, and let me go find Ms. Lake for you." He took off his coat, draped it around her bare shoulders, and started to move toward the gallery again.

"No! No, don't leave me. Please don't leave me alone. Take me home, John, please. I want to…please, I want to go home, take me home." She needed to leave and they were wolves. They were wolves; they were wolves.

She pulled her legs into the limo and shut the door. She felt marginally better when he got into the front seat and under the steering wheel then started the car up and put it into gear. *Home, home, home, home.* Over and over it ran through her mind. *Home.* When she saw that they were headed toward her home and not the hotel, she slid off the seat and onto the floor behind the passenger seat, huddling herself into a ball, and backed herself hard against the door. She glanced up when John rolled the window up between them, hardly aware of the motion, and she didn't move again. It was nearly a two hour ride to the house and her comfort zone. *Home.*

She didn't let her mind go to anything else, but focused on the fact that she was going back home. She would be home soon. She'd think when she got there, but not now. *No, home first, then maybe then I'll think. Maybe.* In the back of her mind, she heard the window between her and John go up and down, but never acknowledged it in any way.

When the limo pulled into her driveway almost two and a half hours later and the engine turned off, she still didn't move. When John opened the door for her, she had to move slowly in order to get out. She was stiff and sore from sitting in one position for so long and her body protested somewhat. When she finally was able to stand up straight, she handed him his coat and hobbled to her door.

"Thank you, John. I'm sorry, but Diana. I forgot about her. You'll need to…" she started to say.

"I've contacted Ms. Lake, Ms. Bennett. I told her I was taking you home. She knows where you are. I'm going back for her now," he told her.

"I…don't bring her here. If she asks you, please…I don't want to see…don't bring her back, please. Not yet, I'll…tell her I'll talk to her soon, but not yet." She wanted them all to go away and never come back. She wanted to be left alone in her misery, left alone with her terrors.

She let herself into the house, locking the locks behind her, and began taking off her clothes as she went. First came the shoes, then the dress. By the time she went past her bedroom door, she was naked, her beautiful clothes strewn out behind her. In the upstairs hallway, she pulled down the attic stairs from the ceiling and went up them. Moving to the back of the rooms up there, she went to a small cubby hole she had made for herself when things became too much, a place she'd been in several times before. She pulled out the six paintings hidden behind old treasures long forgotten and lined them up against the wall.

Chapter Fourteen

The first one, the one she always started with, was of the church. The church her father had wanted to spend his whole lifetime going over and never had the opportunity to. She ran her finger along the buttress of the building in the painting. Since the accident, she had learned all the parts to the church and as much history as she could about the places he had wanted to go to next. She didn't know why, but it had comforted her some, knowing she could pass this bit of information on to the next person. Of course, she didn't see many people, but she had the knowledge anyway.

The next one was the smaller side cemetery they had walked through on that day. Where she had heard the first scream, where she had fallen in her haste to get to them all. She had had to gain special permission to have her father's and brother's ashes buried there. But in the end, they had allowed it. She thought it had more to do with the publicity that she had threatened them with than anything else, but she didn't care. He would have liked knowing she had put them there, she thought, though not for the first time in all these months.

The next one was of Diana being dragged away, the two wolves in full form with their teeth deep into her leg and her side. The detail on this one was perfect, the blood the correct color, the woods behind just turning for fall. She had captured the terror on her face, not that it was hard, she thought. She could see it as if it were only yesterday. Airic touched the woman in this one, ran her finger along her cheek. Her tears blurred her vision for just a moment before she moved on to the next one.

The next two were almost the hardest two to look at, a painting of the horror frozen in time. The first one, the one of her sixteen-year-old brother being torn in half, his legs being pulled one direction, his arms, thin with youth, pulled the other. She stared for long moments at his head; the way his neck was angled left no doubt that it was broken, dead long before they tore at him. She was glad for that, that he didn't suffer long. She wished again that she could ruffle his hair just once more, or hug him to her.

The tears were coming faster now, her heart pounding hard against her breast. Her father was in the next painting. He was forever lying in the damp grasses, arms over his head, his eyes wide open, looking straight at her. The two wolves on him were feasting at his belly, pulling his intestines out of him in long, wet strings and eating them. They had assured her again and again that he had been dead before that, that he hadn't felt any of it. But she knew better; she had seen him turn to her, his mouth form the word "no" to her. Kissing her finger tips, she laid them gently against his face. She could still see the happiness on his face as he had hugged her to him that final time, his excitement of the day. After a whispered, "I love you, Daddy," she sat back against the wall for a few minutes.

The final painting was still turned over facing the wall so that she couldn't see it. She didn't want to turn this one over, hated doing it every time. She didn't know why she kept it, this painting. It hurt her more than the others, so much more. She crawled over on her knees and turned it over then sat back on her heels. It was of him. Him.

The wolves who had taken her told her when she woke up that she was to be the mate to the chosen one, the alpha male, and that she would be honored by all. They bit her daily, both of them shifting in front of her only long enough to tear into her body, deep, bloody wounds, then they would lick them, clean them free of infections. There were always the two, but there had been several others, different ones at least once a day. The pain had been overwhelming, pushing her into darkness even before they were finished tearing into her flesh. They were changing her, they said, preparing her for their leader and their life together. Then on the day before she was brought out of the caves—not a rescue, but damnation; it would never feel like she had been saved—he'd come to her. She would never forget his words or his face.

She lay on the damp cave floor, cold, bleeding and hurt, hurting in every place on her body. He walked in as a wolf, strutted more like it, large and menacing. She cowered back against the cave's cold, damp wall, moving as far back away from him as she could. She knew he was going to bite her, tear into her, and there was nothing she could do. There wasn't anyone to help her.

He didn't say a word to her then sat beside her. When his bite came, she screamed over and over. He had bitten into her soft belly, tossing his massive head back and forth until she would swear his teeth met together through her body. He held on for several minutes then released her; as soon as he slipped his teeth from her, she slipped away, deeper than she'd ever gone.

When she woke, he was sitting there as a man, dressed in a fine suit and tie, as if he hadn't a care in the world. The chair he was sitting in must have been brought in because there had been no furniture in the little cave the whole time she'd been there. She figured that it had been brought in while she was out and it would be taken away once again when he left.

"I've come to claim you. But it is too soon. Tomorrow, I will take you in the way of my kind. I will take you as an animal takes a mate. I will fuck you from behind, take what I need to claim you as my bitch. My alpha bitch." He flicked a tiny fleck of something off his pant leg as he told her, never once looking directly at her. She could have been anyone for all the attention he paid her. Not that she cared, she thought. She wished he would just leave her here.

"Why? Why me?" Her voice croaked and cracked along with her lips that were so dry they too were split and bleeding. She watched as he stood then and walked to her and kicked her in the chest, not hard enough to render her unconscious, but enough to hurt.

"You'll not speak unless I give you permission to do so. I will not tolerate disobedience or disrespect. Why? Because I have been watching you for days and I wanted you. I need no more reason than that. I'm the alpha king and you'll be what I want, do what I say. You will be my bitch and each time you go into heat, I shall impregnate you with my sons. I shall have many sons by you. Heal. I will come for you tomorrow. Be prepared." He stood then and left her there without a backwards glance. As she lay there and cried, the two who had been with her the longest came in and took his chair away. It occurred to her then that he had neither asked her name, nor given her his. She cried for several hours after that and fell into the same nightmare she'd been having since.

Staring at the painting of him now, all she could think of was the small pile of sharp rocks she had gathered to her that night. She had worked hard at getting them sharp enough to stab him, cut at him. She would either kill him or he would kill her in his rage. She hoped for the latter. With each stroke of the rock against another one, she hoped, prayed that he would rip out her throat and leave her alone to die.

She never learned his name, but she would never forget his face.

Chapter Fifteen

Bradley was sitting in his office that same night, about the same time that Airic had sat back away from her paintings and cried herself into a dreamless sleep. He had long since locked up the gallery and was now thinking about all that the woman Diana Lake had told him. Which wasn't much. She was pissed off and very closed-mouthed about her boss.

When Diana had entered the office tonight, he hadn't known what to expect from her or the meeting. She was a little spitfire, he thought. That was for sure. And extremely protective of Airic, or Alastriona, as she had told him her name was.

"What did you say to her? You owe me that much, I think, seeing how you probably won't see either of us again. The way she went out of here, I can assume one of several things right away. You touched her without asking her, or warning her that you were going to touch her causes the same reaction, though not as badly, or you mentioned wolves, werewolves to be precise."

He stared at her. *Well, fuck* was all he could think to say. "I did both, actually. I was angry at her, or at least angry at the situation she caused, and didn't think before I reacted. I've had a really shitty week, not that that excuses what I did, but there you have it. Do I get to know why those two things were at the top of your list? Or why either one would have her tearing out of here like that?" He sat forward in his chair and waited for an answer. He had been insensitive and a jerk, he wasn't ashamed to admit.

"No, you do not. I am not going to tell you what happened to…No, you are not going to get that from me. You don't deserve an explanation because you acted without questions." She rose and he thought she meant to leave, but all she did was walk over to the piece of art that he had treasured for years. "She's been looking for this piece. The buyer wasn't known to us. She won't be happy that you have it, nor will she ask you to sell it to her. "

"You said that you had worked hard to make her come here, why? Or is it because of what you won't tell me?" He watched her looking at the piece, and thinking that if he was in her position right now, he'd knock it over and hope that it broke into thousands of pieces. She studied it for long moments, her face devoid of any emotion she might be feeling. She touched the piece once more and straightened her shoulders, looking as if she had come to a decision, a major one. She turned to him next and he nearly laughed at the expression on her face. It said that she'd love to just rip him to shreds right now.

"When this show is over, Mr. Wolff, I'll expect all the pieces that don't sell to be crated up and her art to be wrapped just as you received them. I'll send a truck for them a week from this Monday; that should give you plenty of time to do both. Also, as I'm planning on staying until the end of the night, I'd appreciate it if you'll stay away from me during this show; right now it is everything I can do not to hurt you physically in some way. But I know that Airic would be pissed if I did." She walked to the door, opened it quietly, and closed it just as quietly.

He had seen her several times throughout the night, always at a distance, talking to the people about the pieces, telling them about the artist. When pressed, she told people that Ms. Bennett had gotten the flu at the last minute and was extremely upset that she couldn't be there tonight. But hopefully, she'd be able to make at least the last couple of nights, maybe if she was better.

She had gotten two phone calls. The first had seemed to upset her. The second, about an hour later, had made a marked difference in her body language. She seemed less stressed, more relaxed, but no less pissed at him if the glares she sent his way were any indication.

Bradley stood and walked over to her "Life Tree," the piece that had made her famous, and the piece that she had been looking for. He ran a finger across it, one of the smooth lines that made it unique from all the other pieces she had done. Finger marks, they were called; the potter's fingers shaping the clay left grooves running up the sides of the piece as it was shaped by her. He pulled out his cell phone, knowing that the other party would be awake.

"Hey, Aaron. I need a favor, can you help me?" He asked Aaron MacManus, his best friend and a vampire.

"Yeah, I can help you out. You want me to bring Sara over so she can slap you around a bit too while we're at it? You know her, always willing to help a friend." Bradley closed his phone. When it rang back, he didn't answer it.

His night was shitty enough without having Aaron's teasing to add to it.

About ten minutes later, Aaron was standing in his office. He just simply appeared there. He had been invited into his house numerous times so coming wasn't a problem. Without saying a word, he walked over to his liquor cabinet and poured them both a whiskey, neat. It wasn't until after taking a seat across from the massive desk and propping his feet on it next to Bradley's that he spoke.

"I've been around for fourteen hundred years and this is the first time since I was turned that I can remember being this relaxed and this happy and it's because of Sara and the twins."

Bradley handed him a cigar out of the box on the desk and took one for him. He had lit them both with the lighter on the desk and taken several puffs before he said anything. "I hurt that woman today. Not physically, but I hurt her nonetheless. I was a jerk and an ass. I don't like the feelings one bit. Here, can you tell me what this says?" He threw a copy of a newspaper article dated over eighteen months ago at him after a few more minutes of careful contemplation.

He had done a Google search on Alastriona Bennett and found several thousand articles about her and her work. The one that caught his attention was an article run by the AP that told about a tragic accident that had taken the lives of her brother and father while they were touring Europe just under two years ago. It glossed over many details, but had hinted that the little family and a friend had gotten off the main path in a wildlife preserve and wild animals had attacked them, killing the two men instantly.

"You want me to read it to you, or just give you details?" Aaron didn't look up from the sheets Bradley had printed off, but read ahead in anticipation of his answer.

"Just the details are okay, thanks. I know that it's in Czech, but does it say that they were in a preserve of some sort?" Bradley leaned back against the chair and waited.

"Preserve? No, it says that Alastriona Bennett was…wait! The artist, this is her? Ah shit, Bradley, you can't be serious. It says that she and her family and a friend were touring the churches of Europe when a pack of wild dogs came from the nearby woods and attacked them. Mr. Bennett Sr. and his sixteen-year-old son were killed during the attack. Shit! Patrick Bennett had had his stomach ripped open and the younger Bennett, Jacob, had his neck broken. It says that the animals had done extensive damage to the two men and positive ID had to be made by dental records sent for from the United States. The women, Diana Lake and Alastriona, had been dragged away by the pack and severely injured. Ms. Lake, it says here, was bitten several times but was found the next afternoon hanging from a tree branch. A professional tracker had been brought in and at press time there was little hope of Ms. Bennett being found alive by anyone on the police force. Well, apparently, they found her alive. Is there anything else?" Bradley tossed the next two sheets over to him.

"ALASTRIONA BENNETT, ARTIST, WAS FOUND TODAY DEEP IN A CAVE NEAR WHERE HER FAMILY REPORTEDLY HAD BEEN

BRUTALLY KILLED SEVERAL DAYS BEFORE. IT WAS FIRST REPORTED THAT THEY HAD BEEN ATTACKED BY A PACK OF WILD DOGS, BUT IT WAS LATER REALIZED THAT IT WAS SOME MIGRATING HOMELESS MEN BENT ON STEALING WHAT THEY COULD NOT GET FOR THEMSELVES HAD THEY HAD A JOB. MS. BENNETT IS WELL KNOWN IN THE UNITED STATES FOR HER WORK IN CERAMICS. SHE WILL BE RELEASED FROM THE HOSPITAL AS EARLY AS DAY AFTER TOMORROW. MS. BENNETT COULD NOT BE REACHED FOR COMMENT."

"Quite a change of venue, don't you think? First you have a poor, tragic family attacked, then its 'she's famous, but not worth bothering for a comment.' I don't buy it. She shouldn't have been that hard to get a comment from. She was in the hospital for Cripe's sake." Aaron put the papers on the desk and leaned back in the chair again.

"Yeah, I can see some bureaucrat being pissed off about having their tourist town advertising that they have a pack of wild animals running around eating the money makers. A few jobs were probably lost over that first article." He took another pull on his cigar. "I don't think it was a pack of wild dogs any more than I suspect you do. I also think maybe I know the tracker." He looked over at Aaron.

"You think it was Bailey. Yeah, I'm sure you're right. If you're thinking it was Bailey, and then you're also right that it was probably werewolves, she'd be pulled in to kill them as well. But to attack like that, is that normal, even for rouges? I mean, the first article says it was early morning when they were attacked, on a tourist route."

Bradley sat up and moved to the vase. "Ms. Bennett was in town the other day. A couple of my wolves…she put them in their place. She's an alpha female. Something isn't right about that; she'd be a rarity without a mate already. I think she was targeted and turned by another alpha male."

Chapter Sixteen

"Fuck! So this alpha male attacks her family, kills them, takes her into this cave, and changes her because…why? I mean, she's beautiful, and obviously talented, but why her?" Bradley knew what he was asking. Why turn a human tourist into a wolf to be an alpha without claiming her?

"The pups from the other day said she was a virgin. And if that's so then he changed her without claiming her. That's also rare and stupid. He wouldn't know if she was his mate without tasting her. And without her being his true mate, there'd be no offspring. Without offspring, there'd be no heir." Bradley had been thinking about the reasons she had been so terrified when she realized she had been with wolves. This newspaper article cleared that up, but opened the door to many other questions as well.

"You can smell when someone is a virgin? Shit, that would be handy, I suppose. So…you and Lynne, that's why there were never any children while you were together. She wasn't your true mate? Okay, but tasting. I didn't know you drank from your partners. I thought you just went at it like bunnies and mated with the one you

79

liked best." *Cocky bastard,* Bradley thought. He knew Aaron knew better than that.

"Yeah, it is handy knowing when a female is a virgin. A virgin is to be treasured, treated with respect. Taking a female's virginity is something we take time with. Not like you vamps who plunder and pillage at first scent, you jackass. And tasting as in tasting her skin; a kiss or even a lick along a vein will do. The taste to us would be like the scent you get that attracts you to your mate. We do bite, though, and taste the blood. It will strengthen the bond between mates and open telepathic pathways between us sometimes. But to turn a human, especially a female human, into one of our kind..." He thought about the pain she would have had to endure. The bites had to be near fatal, brutal in the worst sort of way. The teeth of the biting wolf had to stay in the wound, usually in the soft tissue, for several minutes to ensure that their saliva and enzymes got into the blood stream. That was how the change occurred. In turning a female into an alpha, there had to be a multitude of bites and not all from the same male. The more alpha males that bit her, the stronger the alpha. Most females died after the first bite, but Alastriona hadn't.

"Do you know what her name means? I heard Ms. Lake call her Airic. Her name is Celtic. It means 'agreeable.' That would be a good thing in a mate, I suppose, though not much fun in the long run. Her first name according to the paper is Alastriona. That means 'defends mankind.'"

Both men sat lost in their own thoughts. Bradley was thinking he needed to see her, to apologize to her, grovel.

He had already tracked down her address. John, her limo driver, was one of the members of his pack.

John had said that she sat in the back on the floor huddled in a corner for two hours. And then her first thought, her first concern, was for Diana and how she was going to get home. Yeah, he thought, she would be a great mate for the male that had had her turned. But why not court her, see if she was compatible to him first? It didn't make sense.

"Aaron, why would a man turn a woman without reason? I mean, I can think of thousands of stupid reasons, but why kill her family, turn a perfect stranger, someone you know nothing about, into someone as powerful as an alpha bitch then let her go? Because if the way she handled my pups is any indication, she is one powerful bitch." He was leaning forward on the desk now.

"You think he didn't let her go then. You think he'll come back for her, if he isn't trying to find her already. Hummm, something to think about, I suppose. Let me ask you this, what happens if she's already claimed when he finds her? Do you think he'll walk away?" Bradley hadn't thought of that. He wouldn't, he thought. But then he would have marked her as his too.

"She'll be safe enough, or she will be around here. The only person who could claim her would have to be another alpha; she'd kill any other wolf, pup or adult male. And I'm the only alpha in this pack, in this territory as a matter of fact." After a few seconds, he jerked his head to Aaron. "Oh no, don't even go there. I am not claiming anyone. Been there, done that, and have the t-shirt to prove it. Besides, in case you've forgotten, she sort of hates my guts, and my wolf blood."

His first mate, Lynne, had tricked him into thinking he was her mate by using black magic. She had threatened every female in his pack and the surrounding territories with certain death if one of them went near him. He later figured out it was because she was afraid that one of them could be his true mate and that would end her plans.

She had planned to put him into a situation where he would be challenged and both the males would be killed, making her the alpha of his pack. It happened, but not often. She hadn't counted on Shade, Colin's mate, being a fae being and killing her. Lynne had been sleeping with every male wolf she could, hoping for a pup to claim as Bradley's. Sometimes the sex had not been consensual. It had taken him all this time to regain the trust of some of his pack members again, as she had told them that he was the one making her have sex with them.

"I think you should talk to Bailey and also Mel. Mel might have insider information on this particular style of claiming that you don't know. Bailey and Tristan will be here in a few days to move into their new home. Since she was the first to see her, maybe she could tell you something else about her. I gotta go, it's almost time for the twins to get up for school and that is one thing I will not miss." He dematerialized just as he had appeared; in a flash, he was gone.

Bradley leaned back in the chair again. It would be full moon in two weeks. If he was going to go and see her, it would need to be before then, otherwise he'd miss the pack one here. But she would be alone during the moon phase. Maybe he could romp with her under cover of the moon and she'd never know it was him. That was definitely something to consider.

Chapter Seventeen

She had torn the phone out of the wall two days ago. It had never stopped ringing day and night the four days since the showing. She never carried a cell phone so it wasn't an issue of anyone trying to call her that way. But the courier showing up today with a cell phone completely charged and already on to receive calls was too much. She was so going to fire Diana. When it rang two minutes after she signed the electronic device, and just as the courier was just pulling away, Airic was pretty pissed off. She'd just opened the box, for fuck sake, and she hadn't even gotten back in the studio yet. Pulling it open, she lit into her.

"If this is not a matter of life and death then it will be once I see you again. If you think this is funny, then you are fucking nuts. If you think I'm going to keep this fucking thing once I give you a piece of my mind then you are stupider than the cow grazing in the next field. Oh, and by the way, you're fired, and I mean it this time. You're fired." She was ready to lay into her once again when the voice at the other end spoke.

"What if I just wanted to tell you that it's past time for us to be together? I've waited much too long and I want what I created. I'm coming for you, Airic the artist, have no doubt. You are mine. I told you that before. You will be my mate. We will have sons together. I will be there tonight. You will not run, my dear, or I will be most displeased."

]Airic froze; her breathing ceased to move through her lungs, and her stomach tightened as if would push its meager contents out. She looked up at the new car pulling into the driveway and whimpered. He's here, her mind screamed. He's already here and I can't move.

***

Bradley saw her the minute he pulled into the drive. He had been trying to call her for a couple of days without luck. Just seeing her on the cell phone irked him a little. He'd asked if she had one when he'd had her investigated and had been told no. Damn it, was anything about this woman not complicated beyond reason? He watched her closely as he got out of the car.

The next thing he noticed was she was barefooted and dirty. The next was what he heard her saying "No, no, no, no" over and over again as she backed away from him, her ear still to the phone. He started walking toward her when she dropped the cell phone and pressed herself against the building. Something was wrong; he could hear her softly whimpering. Moving quicker, he was in front of her in seconds.

"Alastriona, what is it? Is it the phone call, is someone hurt?" He bent over and picked up the phone and was handing it to her when she crumpled to the ground. He knelt down to see if she was hurt, and he put the phone to his ear at the same time. "Who is this?" He snapped into the phone. He wasn't trying to be rude, but damn it, she was upset.

"Who is this? Why are you with Airic? She is mine. I made her and she is mine. I will come for her tonight and she had better be prepared if she knows what is good for her. If you wish to live, you will leave her now. I will not tolerate her thinking she can thwart me. I will punish her for this, you tell her that. You should not touch her. You will not touch her. Do you understand me? Tell her to be prepared. I do not tolerate disobedience. I am her…"

"You are shit to her, you worthless excuse for a wolf. Yeah, I know what you are and what you've done. She isn't yours unless you lay claim. You try to find her now, you slimy piece of shit." He closed the phone and slipped it into his pocket. He saw the Fed-Ex bag and pulled it from her limp hand. There was no return address on it. *Well fuck, that would have been too easy,* he thought.

"Alastriona, honey, I need for you to stand up. Look at me, baby. I need for you to stand for me or I'm going to have to pick you up. You can't stay out here in the open, all right?" When she whimpered again, he slipped one arm beneath her bent knees and the other behind her back. "Okay, honey, here we go." Lifting her was simpler than he thought it would be, first because he expected resistance; second because he didn't want to frighten her more than she already seemed to be. He tucked her body into his, pushed open the studio door, and carried her in.

He was surprised by how clean the room was, especially considering how dusty and dirty she was. There wasn't a speck of dirt anywhere. He had assumed his whole life that working with, well, mud that everything would be dirty, or at the very least dusty. But it wasn't. Pieces of her work were everywhere in different stages of completion. He spied another door and as it too was open, he pushed through it and found much of the same, only there was a couch. He took her over to it and set her gently down on it. Pulling the afghan from behind her, he wrapped her in it and then sat down beside her. Looking around the room, he saw a mini-fridge and when he opened it, he found bottles of water. Taking one out and opening it, he went back to her.

"Here, Alastriona, drink this. I need to talk to you. Can you understand me?" He needed to get her somewhere safe and needed her cooperation to do so.

"I'm not stupid, nor am I deaf; of course I can hear you. If you've come here to yell at me again, then get it over with and leave. I apparently have plans for the night." She moved closer to the corner of the couch and further away from him.

Grinning, he leaned back to look at her. She wasn't as pale, but she was covered in white dots. When he pulled one out of her hair, it crumbled in his fingers. "What is this stuff? You have it all through your hair." She was looking at him now, well, glaring would be a better description, and he was shocked. *My God,* he thought, *she's beautiful. Not just beautiful, but amazingly, incredibly beautiful.* It took him several moments to realize she was saying something else to him.

"I'm sorry, what did you say? I seem to have lost my train of thought." Looking into her eyes that were the color of rich, dark chocolate, he waited for her to answer.

"I asked if you are here to take me to him. Because if you are, I'm afraid I'm going to have to decline." He looked down at her hand when he felt the gun barrel poke him in the stomach.

Chapter Eighteen

Bradley raised his hands up so that she could see that they were empty. He glanced again down at the gun and saw that it was a Colt .45, an older one at that. He couldn't smell any gunshot residue, nor could he detect any silver.

"Alastriona, this is not the route you want to go. I'm not here to take you to him; in fact, now that I have found you, I'm sworn to protect you. Put the gun away and let's talk about this." He had to work to make his voice sound as if he wasn't afraid she'd shoot him.

"Protect me. You? I think not. I'd like you to go away, please. I have this, and I will shoot him when he comes here." She stood up and waved the gun toward the door.

The second the gun was no longer pointed at him, he reached out and snatched it from her hand, disarming her as quickly as that. He opened the cylinder with one hand and emptied the casings into his other hand. He put the shells into his trouser pocket and snapped the cylinder back into the frame. He put the gun onto the table at the side of the couch. Ten seconds and she was completely disarmed.

"You bastard. Why are you here? I want you to get out of my house right now. I don't want you here. It's not safe, not even for me." She walked over to the door and opened it for him.

"You wouldn't have been able to kill him with that anyway, you know. There isn't any silver in the shells and there are only six shots, not enough to kill someone with an alpha's power. But he would have had you disarmed as quickly as I did, and you'd have only succeeded in pissing him off more." He didn't move. He couldn't leave her, not now. He watched her for a minute when something occurred to him. "You weren't going to kill him; that was your plan, you were just going to piss him off. You want him to destroy you."

"Leave, don't leave, I don't care either way." He watched as she walked out of the room and back into the yard. He stood to follow her and pulled out his cell phone at the same time. Time was running out and he needed to get her to somewhere safe.

"Hello, Bradley, how's the meeting going? Has she made you grovel much? Sara had me crawl on my knees because I said something stupid to her the other night. It was quite fun. We had to…"

"Aaron, I need, can you meet me here? Remember the discussion we had about the other alpha? Well, when I got here she was on the phone with him. He had sent her a phone in order to contact her to tell her he was coming for her. And…well, she pulled a gun on me as well. She plans to have him destroy her instead of claim her." He didn't know what she was doing or where she was going, he just knew that he needed to get to her. He walked out to follow her, even if all he had was her scent.

"Yes, I'll come to you, you know that. When did this happen, just today? Maybe we could get Pete to look at the phone and see what she can find out. May I bring her as well?" He could hear the seriousness in his voice and appreciated him all the more for his friendship.

"I was hoping you could help me convince Alastriona to come to the pack house with me. And if that fails, help me subdue her. It will piss her off, but she can be pissed off at the house with several other wolves around to help keep her safe. She's one of mine now and I protect what is mine." He had heard Aaron say the same words many times over the years they had known each other and he finally understood what he meant.

"Five minutes. Oh, and if you think she'll only be pissed, well, I wouldn't want to be in your shoes when she gets there." Bradley could hear his laughter as he hung up.

By the time he hung up, he was at the back door of her home. Trying the knob and finding it locked, he simply pushed against the jamb with his shoulder and popped the door's lock. There was no way she was staying here, not if he had anything to say about it. He opened the door and simply walked in.

Bradley prided himself on his ability to be quick on his feet. It was a good thing too because no sooner had the door opened than she had him thrown to the floor. He didn't want to hurt her so he was careful how he handled her, but it soon became obvious that she was going to hurt him if he didn't take a more aggressive stance against her.

He flipped her over onto her back, pulled her hands above her head with his hands, and trapped her body at her hips beneath his, this only because he was stronger physically and he outweighed her by nearly fifty pounds.

"Stop this right now. Damn it, Alastriona, you're going to hurt yourself if you don't stop." She continued to struggle against this hold until he leaned down and bit gently into her shoulder.

Chapter Nineteen

It was a wolf's submissiveness move, the neck being the most vulnerable part of the body besides the belly. Biting this way showed her he was the aggressor and she needed to submit to him or he'd bite her harder until she did. She stilled immediately; her entire body became stiff.

Bradley had an overwhelming need to taste her, the conversation he'd had with Aaron forgotten, and his claim that he was never mating again gone from his memory.

He licked his tongue across the skin that was caught between his teeth and moaned. He released the holding bite, moved his mouth along her bare shoulder, and nuzzled his mouth against the point of her neck that met the shoulder. He kissed the warm, silky skin and nipped at the pulse beating there. Need, his need to mate, dominated his thought process completely.

He felt her move beneath him, her fingers gripping his hand. Moving his mouth lower, he followed the vein along her throat, then he stopped at the base of her neck. Her own moan vibrated along her throat against his mouth. He ran his hands down her arms, caressing them as he went. His tongue licked the area there, taking more of her taste into his mouth. His body leaned closer to her and his legs tightened around her as he gently covered her with his length. He ran his tongue up the length of her neck, moving along her hot blood as he went.

When his mouth met her jaw, he moved up and gently swept his mouth against hers, brushing his lips across the fullness of hers, the heat. Once, then again, breathing her in as he went back and forth until he felt her respond to him. He nipped at her bottom lip and suckled it into his mouth, pulling more of her flavor in. He pulled back an inch and looked into her eyes, waiting for her to look back at him.

When their eyes met, Bradley slowly moved the last inch to her mouth and rocked against her core with his cock. Moving his right hand down her ribs, he slipped it beneath her, spreading his hand wide, pressing her to him. His left hand moved to her head, angling her head, and held her to him as he kissed her. His mouth covered hers as he rolled over and brought her body over his, cradling her between his legs.

He moved his hands down her ribs and cupped her ass, pulling her tight against his hard cock. Moaning deep, he reached further, never breaking contact with the sweetness of her mouth, and grasped her thighs. Tugging her up and widening her legs, he settled them along his own hips this time. When she moved against him on her own, began riding him, he sat up, bringing her with him; they were chest to chest now.

Grasping her hips, he moved her faster and harder against him. He slipped his hand to the hem of her shirt, pulled it up over her head, and tossed it aside. He felt her fingers move along the buttons of his shirt as he cupped her breast, still covered in the scrap of material of her bra. Pressing them together, he ran his thumb over the stiff peaks of her nipples as she ran her fingers through the hair on his chest.

"Alastriona, baby. I want to suckle; I need to suckle your breast in my mouth." His voice had deepened; he felt that as much has he heard it.

"Yes...I, please. Please, Bradley." She gripped his shoulders and lifting one leg up then the other, she wrapped them around his hips, anchoring her ankles at his back, and began riding him harder, tighter with his help.

Bradley pushed her breast up until it spilled out of the bra and bounced slightly. Her nipple was pink and tight. As much as he wanted to savor the sight, need pushed him forward and he took her into his mouth and suckled. Sucked hard and firmly, pulling the tight nub in as deeply as he could. When he scraped his teeth gently over the swollen peak, he drew a tiny drop of blood. As he licked the tiny wound, tasting her, Alastriona tossed back her head and came apart, screaming her sudden release.

He held her to him as she began to settle, his body screaming for its own release, but not here, he thought, not on the kitchen floor. He wasn't going to take his mate for the first time on the floor. Because after his first taste of her skin, the first lick across her warmth, he knew he'd found his true mate. Before he could lift her up and take her to her bed, he heard someone pounding at the front door.

Aaron. He'd completely forgotten about his friend. Then he remembered the man on the phone. Her life was in danger and here he was acting like they hadn't a care in the world, like a randy pup. Some mate he'd turn out to be if someone took her before he could claim her. He gently pulled her away from him and stood, reaching down to help her up as well. She heard the doorbell now, pealing along with the pounding, and stood as well. Her knees must have been a little wobbly because she leaned heavily back against the counter for support.

"It's my friend Aaron; I asked…he's here to help me get you home. Hummm, I…I'll go let him in." She was breathing hard; her breasts still cupped above the bra were heaving enticingly so. He backed up two steps and before he could pull her to him again, he turned and went to the front of the house.

"Someone is coming. Hurry, we need to get out of here now," Aaron said as he opened her door.

Chapter Twenty

Alastriona stood in the kitchen and listened to the men in the other room. She could hear them as if they were standing next to her. They couldn't make her go anywhere, she thought, not if she didn't want to. She didn't care who was coming.

After putting her clothes back in order, she reached into the refrigerator and pulled out the jug of iced tea. The ice machine in here was always full, so after filling a glass with the icy chunks, she poured herself some and sat down at the kitchen table. What had she done?

Before she left for the gallery opening, she had made a call to a local cleaning service and had set up someone to come in three times a week. She told them that she wanted them to send someone who would cook a few meals, nothing fancy, so that she could eat something besides toaster tarts and plain pasta. In the week since she had started working for her, Maggie was doing a great job. The tea was a nice bonus too.

As soon as she settled down, she began to think again. She had just almost had sex with a wolf. An alpha wolf, if he hadn't lied to her at the showing. Right here in her kitchen, on the flipping floor no less. She looked over where they had been and thought of his mouth on hers and how hard he had been between her legs, how good it had felt. She could still feel his length pressing into her softness, the way his mouth felt...she slammed the lid down on that train of thought. This was getting her nowhere, damn it.

She wasn't going to blame him; she had wanted him as much as she thought he did her. She'd never had sex before, never wanting to waste her time on what she thought to be a ridiculous pastime. But deep down, she knew that it may have been with anyone else, which because it was him, it had been so...fuck! Mind, stay focused, she groused.

She looked up at her problem leaning against the door jamb leading from the living room, grinning like an idiot.

"Have you worked it all out yet?"

He was laughing at her, she realized, and she wasn't sure why, but it pissed her off. "Worked out what? And I don't know who you think you are, or that guy at the door, but I'm staying here. This is my house, and I'm not going anywhere with any of you people." She folded her arms over her chest and glared at him.

"You seemed to be trying to work out the problems of the world when I walked in. It was kinda cute, really. And about him, could you come in here and ask him in? He can't cross your threshold without your permission." She sat there for all of five seconds and stood to go into the front.

"What are you, some sort of vampire or something? You need my permission to gain entrance to...whatever, you're not welcome. Go away, both of you, go away." She looked at the man standing just outside her door. He was one of the men from the gallery, and up close he was more gorgeous and sexy-looking. Not as good-looking as the wolf, but really nice, she decided.

"Yes. Yes, I am a vampire, Airic. Will you let me in, please? You're in trouble here, and Bradley has asked me to help."

She realized in that moment that he was, he really was a vampire, and he wanted in her home. There was a vibe about him, strength and power, not just because of his size, but something else, something she could taste about him.

"Why? I mean, I'm not going to let you bite me, unless of course it's to drain me. You can do that, right? Drain a person to death? I think we could work out something. I...yes, that would work out for both of us. I let you in, you kill me. Fair trade, I think." It would be all right, she guessed. She'd read books, smut books actually, that said a vampire's bite was very sexual, erotic. Maybe if she had another orgasm like the one in the kitchen with fur ball, she could die a happy woman.

"He's not going to kill you, no one is. Not as long as I'm alive. Ask him in, Alastriona. We have to get you going to the pack house." He moved to stand just in front of her, as if to protect her from the vamp, she thought.

"I believe I've told you this before, Alpha King, or whatever you are, I'm not going anywhere. So if you'll just give me my bullet thingies, I'll tuck my gun in the back of my pants and make this the Alamo. Mr. Aaron, sorry you had to waste your time, but I'm not..." She felt the touch at her elbow seconds before she weakened, her body going limp. Turning as she fell into Bradley's arms, she saw the woman. "I didn't give you…" It was too much effort to form words, but she knew the pretty woman got it.

"I don't need permission like he does. I'm sorry about this, but you're much stronger than I thought. Sleep now, Alastriona Airic Bennett, sleep."

Her eyes got heavy, and then she felt herself slip away.

Chapter Twenty-One

"She's not here, my lord. We cannot go into the residence, as someone has put a ward around it. I can sense a bit of magic, but not much, at least not surrounding the house. What would you like for us to do now?" Peter asked him.

Christopher Felix Alastair, alpha wolf, leaned back in his seat. He had told her not to leave, forbidden it as a matter of fact. She would need to learn who her master was, and he would enjoy showing her, once he found the bitch.

"Set six wolves to patrol the area and have them notify me as soon as she comes home. Please make sure they know not to touch her or I will kill them slowly, very slowly." He sounded bored, but inside, he was seething. He knew her disappearance had something to do with the man on the phone. He had told those fools in Europe to kill the males in her family, and they had obviously missed this one. Heads would roll for this, literally. *No matter,* he thought, *I will enjoy taking care of that one myself.*

"My lord, the alpha in this territory, he will know that we are here. Should I contact him and let him know why we are here?" Christopher turned slowly and looked at his man.

"Do you presume to tell me my business, Peter? I certainly hope not; that would be most unwise of you. It would be a shame to lose one with such caliber as yours this late in the game. Death for one such as yourself would be…sad, don't you think? And your own poor mate…what would become of her?" He watched as Peter paled at the reminder that he wasn't the only one beholden to him.

"No, my lord. I'm sorry, my lord. I'll make sure the patrols are set up and they know your wishes. All will be as you wish." Peter bowed again and backed away, still bent at the waist.

"Oh, Peter. I just realized that we should contact the alpha in this territory and let him know that we have a runaway wolf. Please contact him for me and let him know that we will take care of the dangerous wolf with care, the dangerous male wolf. Run along now, you have plenty to keep yourself busy." Peter moved away without another word.

He had hoped that Peter would make a fuss, any noise to indicate that he was displeased with him, but he hadn't. He loved pushing the man to his limits. The last time had been so much fun, but he'd have to be more careful next time. Punishing his mate to near death had been a mistake, a fun one, but a mistake all the same. And Christopher hated making mistakes.

He thought about the woman, the alpha bitch he had created. She was just what he needed. He had watched her and her family for days before he'd made his decision. He had thought to take the littler one of the two, but didn't like the way she kept walking behind the fatter one. That would not do for an alpha bitch, his alpha bitch, to walk behind anyone.

The fat one, Airic he had learned later, would suit better. He would never worry about her leaving him, he thought. She would be grateful that someone like him had taken the time to change her into something better and keep her. If she proved not suitable for his purposes, then he would simply kill her as he had the others. He wanted a son, lots of sons as a matter of fact, and the foolish women would not breed him one no matter how hard he had tried.

Christopher had the driver take him to the nearest open area. He needed a run, a hard run and maybe a kill. Oh yes, he thought, a nice kill would make me feel so much better.

When the limo pulled into a parking space at the nature persevere, he got out of the car and looked around. He could smell the burning meat on the grills and his stomach turned. He much preferred his meat raw, and the bloodier the better. He could also smell humans, not too many, but enough. Smiling, he began to loosen his tie and remove his Alexander Amosu suit. He did not believe in shifting while dressed, and certainly not in a hundred thousand dollar suit. The nine 18-carat gold and pave set diamond buttons helped set this suit apart from all others, which was just the way he liked to be, apart.

After shifting into his wolf, a massive beast that had never been mistaken for anything like a dog, he ran into the woods.

He ran full out for perhaps twenty minutes before he began to track his prey. It was full dark now, but he could see as well in this light as he could in full day. Raising his muzzle to the air, he sniffed. *Ah,* he thought, *there she was,* her fresh blood making it almost too easy for him to track her. He could smell the others, one a mate, the other a small female. He only wanted the woman, but if the others proved to be too difficult, then so be it, two less humans in the world.

Moving along the path they were walking on, he watched her. She had fallen and her knee was bloody and raw, giving him the scent to track. She was laughing now, teasing the male about how silly she'd been falling like a child.

Christopher didn't want her laughing; he wanted her terror, her fear. The taste of those emotions made the blood far richer than any other he could think of. His needs, the need to taste nearly made him leap at her too soon.

The man sat down on a log and looked up at his prey. When the small human moved to be picked up, Christopher moved quickly and lunged at her as she was bending over. His massive jaws were biting into her waist and startling a scream from her. Momentum from the combination of his weight and the jump had him pulling her away before the man could react. Within seconds, he had her pulled deep into the forest, her screams rending the air.

When he had her far enough away, he bit harder, rendering her unconscious and quiet, at least for now. He shifted and picked her up, throwing her over his shoulder, and took off running. Even as a human, he could run quickly and quietly.   He needed to get her away without leaving a trail to follow.

His cock was hard and straining with need when he dropped her on the floor of the cave he had found. He was going to fuck her, fuck her hard, and pretend it was his mate. The need to punish was great and he loved to fuck people as a punishment. Male or female, it mattered little to him. Power was what he wanted and felt he got that when he dominated by using sex over them. Christopher wanted her awake, but his need was too strong. He flipped her over onto her stomach and pulled her ass up to meet him, uncaring of the wounds he'd inflicted and the blood.

Without any preparation at all—what did it matter? She was as good as dead anyway—he slammed his huge cock deep into her ass. The tight hole nearly sent him over the edge, and her screams ripped through him, making him thicker, harder within her. Yes, he thought, this was what being an alpha was about, dominance, power and dominance. Running his hand along the gaping wound, he gathered blood and rubbed it along his chest and over her ass. Moving faster now, he held her tight against him, enjoying her struggle to get away almost as much as he did smelling her fresh blood. He was close, so close he could feel his balls tighten against his cock. Leaning over, he elongated his jaw to his wolf and bit into her shoulder deep and hard, making her scream again and again. It was perfect, he thought as he shot his cum deep into ass, absolutely perfect. As the last of his seed spilled into her, her screams still echoing in the cave, he reached around to her neck and snapped it, killing her instantly.

Chapter Twenty-Two

Airic woke in a dark room. There were candle everywhere, some of them lit, and it helped take away the shadows in the corners. She had no idea where she was, but she had a pretty good idea who had brought her here because this was not her house. She was going to have a word or two with that fucking ass as soon as she found him. She started making a mental list as she moved the covers off her body. Quickly, she threw them back over her. She was naked.

"I thought you'd sleep better with them off. I certainly enjoyed removing them for you. Maybe next time you could take mine off as well." He was here with her. *Fuck! Fuck! Fuck!*

"There won't be a next time, you arrogant ass! Where are my clothes? And when you tell me, I want you to leave so I can get dressed to go home. This is stupid; didn't you ever do what someone told you as a kid? Probably not, I'm betting. What are you doing sitting there still? Give me my clothes and get out." She saw him move, no, not move, glide toward her. His body was like liquid sex, she thought, and she mentally slapped her forehead to get herself back on track.

"I can read your thoughts. I've tasted you, you see. And once you taste me, my blood, you'll hear mine as well. Right now I'm glad you can't read them. I'm sure you don't want to know what wicked thoughts are running rampant through there." She watched as he sat down on the side of the bed, scooting closer to her each time she moved away. When the blankets had her trapped on the one side and him on the other, he reached down and brushed his finger lightly across her cheek. She just managed to stop the moan before it escaped her lips.

"Don't. Please don't. I want to...please stop...I need...where are my...oh yes." He kept touching her; she couldn't think when he did that. And her friggin' body wouldn't listen. Her mouth kept telling it, "no, no," but the mind and body were saying, "fuck yeah! Let the party begin!"

She felt the blanket move down her chest just before he licked the traitorous nipple, pulling it deep into his mouth. Her body arched up into his mouth.

"I want you, Alastriona. I want to make love to you." He moved to the other breast as he spoke and nibbled the other nipple to a near painful peak. She couldn't stop the moan this time. Her mind had won and her body was going full steam ahead.

"You...don't do...stop, please...oh more, please more." He had moved to lie beside her now, taking full advantage of the fact that she was trapped. Not that it mattered anymore. She was moving toward him now, not away.

She helped him, helped him push the soft blanket down her body. She wanted him to touch her, to lick her, taste her. She wanted to do the same to him as well and moved to touch his bare skin. She realized then that he was naked as well, and that he was erect, very hard.

Alastriona had never slept with anyone before, but she had seen naked men, mostly in art class, using the male form as a model. But he was different. He was muscled and hard, but his skin was silky and tight. And hot. Everywhere she touched him she felt his heat. Moving her hands down his hard abs, she ran her fingers through the coarser hair just below his belly button.

"Baby, if you keep this up, this won't last as long as I'd like for it to." He had captured her wandering hands and kissed them both before placing them on his chest. "Here for now. Touch me here." Pulling her closer to him, he kissed her.

This kiss wasn't like the others; this one felt more possessive, hungrier. He demanded entrance this time, his tongue sliding along her lips and pushing inside when she opened to him. He moaned deep. She felt it rumble along her body. He pressed her back against the mattress and covered her body with his heavy weight.

His hand moved down her ribs and then along her ass, pulling her hard and up into him. She could feel the hardness of his cock through the blanket, and she slid her leg up his to hook around him, but wasn't able to because of the stupid blankets.

"Christ, I want you. You're hot and I can smell you, your arousal. I need to taste you, now, I need to taste." He began to move down her body, licking and nipping at her as he went. By the time he had settled himself between her legs, she was wild with a need of her own.

She leaned up on her elbows as he sat on his feet. His cock was hard and sticking straight out from his groin. As she watched him, he wrapped his hand around the shaft and pumped his hand up and down. A drop of cum seeped from the tip. She licked her lips, a need to take him into her mouth making her hungry and aggressive. She started forward, reaching for him, and he stopped her.

"No. Not yet. I would like nothing better than to have you wrap your mouth around me, but I want to taste you more. Next time, I promise you'll be able to do what you want, but next time. Oh, sweetheart, you're wet, so wet I can see the dampness on your curls." He let go of his cock and touched her pussy. As much as she wanted to roll her eyes in the back of her head, she knew instinctively that he wasn't finished.

His finger moved slowly along her nether lips, up and down like he had done to his cock. Her body responded and she felt her pussy weep more. He hadn't touched her yet, not touched her where she needed. When his finger slowly entered her heat, she opened her legs wider and raised her hips up to meet him.

"Please, Bradley. I want you. I...there's a need, something...I don't... you have to fill it for me, please, fill me." Her hips moved up and down with his finger and when he inserted another into her, she nearly came up off the bed. Whimpering now, she moved faster with his fingers.

"I need to stretch you, love. You're too tight to take me inside of you yet. That's what you want, me to fill you with my cock, isn't it?" He was moving faster now. Her body was on fire.

"Yes, oh yes, please." She felt rather than saw him move, her body straining to get to something. When she felt his breath on her thigh, she started to clamp her legs closed, but he held them open with his hands. She was panting now, her need making her ache for release.

With his fingers, he opened her lips and ran his tongue inside her, lapping at her, tasting her. When his mouth closed over her clit and suckled it into his mouth, she screamed out her climax, but he didn't stop. While his fingers fucked her, his mouth teased and nipped at her until she came again and again.

"Please, Bradley, please. I want you; I want to suck your cock. Now, I want you to come in my mouth." As she reached for him, pulling away from his very talented tongue, she pushed him back against the footboard. She leaned forward and stroked the length of him with just the tips of her fingers; his hiss made her bolder.

"Take me, love. Take me in your mouth. I want to fuck your hot mouth and shoot cum deep into your throat."

She swiped her tongue across the tip of the large, deep purple head, taking the cream into her mouth. He hissed again. Bolder than she had ever been in her life, she wrapped her lips around him and licked again. She loved the way he responded, pumped into her. She didn't know what she was doing, but taking her cues from him and his body, she licked and nipped every inch of him, up one side of him then down the other. She felt his hand touch the back of her head, felt him guide her, show her what he needed. Soon he was pumping into her hard, his cock bumping the back of her throat again and again.

"I'm going to come, Alastriona. Fuck, I'm coming!" Seconds later, she felt the first hot explosion hitting the back of her throat. He pumped harder into her, pulsing into her over and over. She swallowed him, his cum, loving the salty taste that she knew was unique to him. He lifted her up and turned her over onto her hands and knees. She was ready, she thought, so ready for his cock to be deep inside of her. Moaning, she moved back against him. Then she felt him stiffen behind her, felt his anger roll off him and into her.

Then she heard it. Pounding again, at the door. No, she thought, no, no. He leaned down and pulled her up to him. With his cock hard against her back, he held her tight to him.

"I have to go. I'm so sorry. You have no idea how sorry. But I have to go see what's wrong." He moved to the side of the bed, stood up, and looked back at her. She could see the regret in his eyes. She huddled under the covers and hid. But it didn't stop her from hearing the man at the door.

"A wolf just attacked a woman in the nature preserve about seventy miles from here. The husband and child weren't hurt. David is organizing a search party now."

Chapter Twenty-Three

She wanted to hide, but knew that she couldn't. She also knew that it was him, the man from the phone, the one who had said he'd come for her. When he couldn't find her, he had punished someone else.

Alastriona got up and made the bed. It took her nearly fifteen minutes because it was so big and they had made a royal mess of it. As soon as she was finished, she went into the bathroom.

It was huge! Along with all the normal bathroom needs there was a shower stall that would easily hold four people with jets at two levels and overhead. The thing she thought she'd enjoy the most was a deep, sunken bath tub. The tub was surrounded with a large shelf that was filled with ferns and unlit candles in silver and glass holders. One whole wall was glass blocks that would let the light in during the day. Overhead and centered over the tub was a skylight. It was still dark enough that the moon and stars were visible in it. Sighing heavily, she turned on the shower. Using his things felt very personal and intimate. Trying not to dwell on that too much, she hurriedly washed her hair and her body and was drying off in record time. Finding her clothes proved to be futile.

After looking for a good thirty minutes, she finally had to open one of his drawers and wear a shirt of his. There were only white t-shirts in any of the drawers, and being a female with large breasts, she knew that white and her darker nipples just wouldn't...well, it just wouldn't. Going through another drawer, she found several pair of boxer shorts and finding the smallest-looking ones she could, slipped them on. Next, she went to the closet. She didn't want to wear one of his nice shirts, but that was all she could find. *He must not ever wear fun clothes,* she thought. Too bad, a very tight tee and some equally fitting jeans made her mouth water just thinking about it. After pulling on a pair of his socks, she went downstairs.

The house was bigger than she thought and she wandered about the main floor for a few minutes before she heard the voices. Following them, she ended up in the kitchen where several other women were. They all stopped talking and turned to stare when she opened the door.

"Hello, I was wondering where my clothes might be?" The quietness of the room was loud and overwhelming.

A pretty, very pregnant woman came to stand before her and then dropped to her knees. And started rubbing her neck against her leg.

"I'm so sorry, mistress, I forgot them. The alpha said to wash them and have them back in your rooms as soon as possible, but I was...I have no excuse. Please forgive me?"

"What are you doing? Get up! I can do my own friggin' laundry. Here, let me help you." Alastriona leaned over to help the woman up to her feet. She had been shocked when she dropped like that. Guiding her to a chair, she helped her sit down. Pulling out another chair, she picked her legs up and sat them gently on the seat. She looked around the room and noticed the look of amazement on the other faces, but barely registered it. "What's your name, please?" She nodded to a woman about her age.

"Megan Sheppard, mistress," the girl answered. Alastriona saw her back up several tiny steps as she answered. *And I thought I was timid,* she thought.

"Megan, could you please get me a large bucket? And stop calling me mistress; it's just Airic, or Alastriona, but I prefer Airic." She watched curiously as Megan looked quickly to the older woman in the group and with her small nod, left to get the bucket, she hoped. "My mother carried my little brother...my little brother Jacob in the summer. He would have been eighteen this year." Airic moved to the sink and turned on the cold water tap. She stared out the window over the sink and continued. "I'm sorry, I was drifting. She had swollen feet and legs like you do. The doctor was forever telling her to sit down and put her feet up, but her hips hurt doing that. My dad is, err was an engineer and he watched her struggle with it. He searched on the Web for over a week on what could help her. Then one day, he tried cold water. He had her soak her feet and ankles in cold water. Thank you." Megan had brought the bucket and she began to fill it with the cold running water. When the bucket was about half full, she carried it over to the young woman and had her plunge her feet into it. She grinned when the girl sighed.

"That does feel good. Oh so very good. Thank you, mis…Airic." It was then that she realized she didn't know her name.

"You're very welcome. What's your name and when are you due?" Airic wanted to touch the mound at her belly, but knew that some women found that to be an intrusion into their personal space. Nor would she ask her.

"Donna Wolff, and I'm due in three weeks. I'm David Wolff's mate." She said that as if Airic should know, but she didn't comment. She didn't know any of them and would most likely be gone in a few hours anyway. Maybe forever if that man found her. "Would you like to feel him?"

Airic looked at the woman and nodded. She couldn't form any words; her throat had locked up. Stretching out her shaking hand and let Donna take it and place it over her baby. The kick startled her, and when it seemed to roll under her hand seconds later, Donna laughed.

"Doesn't that hurt?" She felt her face blaze hot with embarrassment. And she went to pull her hand away, but Donna only held it tighter to her.

"No, it doesn't hurt. It feels great to know there's life inside of me. You'll have your own soon enough, a son for the alpha."

Airic jerked away and stood. A son. That man had said she would have his sons, many sons. He had hurt a woman, probably killed her because of her. She backed to the wall and stared at them all. What if he came here? She noticed then that there were several pregnant women in the room, about three more.

"I have to go. He'll come…my clothes, where…where is the laundry room?" She was hyperventilating now, and she was dizzy. Holding on to the counter, she moved to the door and outside. Run, she had to run away. There was no way she would let that man come here.

"Alastriona, Alastriona, listen to me. Stop right now. Damn it, girl, I'm too old to have to shift and run after you, but I will."

Chapter Twenty-Four

"He'll come here, that man. He'll find me here and hurt those nice women. I have to go, leave. I…my home. I'll go to my home." Airic stopped and let the older woman catch up to her, but she still moved backwards and away from her.

"And what do you think will happen if you go home? Do you think that he will happily take you into his arms and love you? And what do you think Bradley will do when he finds you missing from here? Do you think he'll just let you go, not come after you and bring you back here?"

She glared at the woman. What was it any of her business anyway? "I'm my own person. And do you think I care what he'd do to me over what I have seen? What he could do to those women in there, or those children they carry? Bradley? He said that I'm his responsibility because I'm in his territory, nothing more. Well that's easily remedied, isn't it? I can throw anywhere." Airic looked longingly at the trees. Whenever she got upset, for some reason, walking in the trees soothed her. She turned back to the older woman.

"I can't let you run, Airic. Bradley's my grandson and my alpha. Letting you run away would tear him apart. You must know that. He has looked a long time for you, and now that he's found you, he won't let you go that easily. None of his people will. Not now." She had wrapped her arm around Airic's waist and was guiding her to a group of chairs that were set up around a large in-ground pool.

"Look, I'm not sure what you think is going on between us, but it isn't permanent. I mean he…that is, we haven't…I'm just someone he wants to have…sex, that's all it is, just sex. I'm sure that he'd have no problem getting anyone, and I mean anyone, to sleep with him. The couple of times we've almost…you know, he seems to know his way around a body pretty well, so there'd be no complaints about that. But I have to go home. I'm…you know not experienced enough to keep someone like him happy." Airic looked at the woman and saw that she was shaking with laughter. Frowning, she started at her. "What the hell…heck is so funny?"

Laughter burst from her then. She had to lean forward and hold her belly she was laughing so hard. Airic watched her and never said a word. These people are nuts, certifiable.

"Oh God, child, you are too much. You will talk about having sex with my grandson with me, but you won't cuss. That's just too funny. Oh my, I don't believe I've laughed that hard in a coon's age." Airic watched Mrs. Wolff wipe tears from her cheeks and sighed.

"I didn't say we had sex, I said he was good with a body. And my mother would have tanned my butt but good if I'd cursed in front of an elder." She sat there for several minutes and looked over the pool. The water looked so smooth, she thought, smooth like Bradley's body sliding against hers. She sat up suddenly. Thoughts like that were not going to help her get home.

"You don't know what you are, do you, love?" Seeming to have gotten control of herself again, Mrs. Wolff leaned back and looked at her.

"I'm an animal. That wolf, the one that attacked that woman tonight, he's a werewolf too. He hurt her because he couldn't find me. He'll keep hurting until he gets what he feels is his. Me." She didn't want to see the certain blame in her eyes, so Airic kept looking at the water.

"Probably. Do you know who he is? If so, then you could help them find him and punish him by telling Bradley. The men who left here tonight, they'll search until they find her, if that's what worries you. But you don't think they'll find her alive, do you?" Mrs. Wolff asked her.

"No. They won't. When those men had me in that cave, they brought in another woman. She was very young and she screamed continuously. They told me that the master had told them they were not to touch me, but that didn't mean they couldn't touch others. The bigger one said that I had to watch them while they played, I had to be prepared, he had told me. He raped her first while the others held me still. Then they took turns with her, holding me so that I could see what they did to her. Then when they finished, they tore her in two, literally ripped her in half and tossed her beside me. She laid there for a whole day before they took her body away." She looked at her now, turning in her seat. "He'll not stop. I don't know why I know that, but I do. He said that he wanted me and that was reason enough to kill my family. He still thinks he owns me now because he created me. I'll talk to Bradley when he returns, but I won't stay." Airic stood then and walked back to the house. She felt Mrs. Wolff following her and held the door open so that she could enter before her. "When the men return, they'll be tired and hungry. I think we should fix them a big breakfast and have it ready when they get here. Mrs. Wolff, do you know how many men went and maybe give me an idea of what they'll eat?" Airic pulled out a sheet of paper and began making notes.

***

They found her body four hours after the call from David. It had taken them longer because when he shifted to carry her off, they had lost his scent and had to backtrack to find another trail. She was dead, as Airic had said she'd be. Her body had been torn at and ripped to pieces. Bradley stood over her as he waited for the others to arrive.

He had already sent six pack members as wolves to follow the two scents out of the cave to see if they could find where he had gone when he left. He didn't think it would do any good, but he had to try.

He kept thinking about Alastriona and what she had endured at this monster's hand. She hadn't been killed, but she would have suffered terribly. She had been in the cave as a captive for six days and nights until Bailey found her. Bailey had told him she had begged to be left there, to tell the others that she hadn't found her. But of course she hadn't. Even after almost two years, Bailey said that she could still smell him in the room and on her. She said that Alastriona was extremely strong to have endured what she had.

He moved to the mouth of the cave when he felt David draw near. He was in human form, as were the rest of the pack members. Because of the other officers on his force who where humans, David played the human when he needed to. Bradley and the others did as well. It made for good working relations when they didn't think of you as a movie-type werewolf.

"Thanks, Bradley, I appreciate the help. Is she dead? Yeah, thought so." They watched the coroner's van pull up the hill toward them. "This isn't going to be good you know?"

"Yeah, I know. We have to find him and soon." Bradley had already told David about Airic and the phone. He hadn't had a chance to tell him she was his mate, though. He wasn't ready to share that yet, just a little nervous about the fact that they still had not mated.

He had dropped off the cell phone to Pete yesterday to have her see what she could find out about it. Pete was a computer whiz and could find out anything legal or illegal about anyone when she set her mind to it. She was also a magical being, a wood nymph, and mated to Dominic, Chief of Security and bodyguard to Aaron.

"So, you gonna tell me about my new alpha bitch, or do I gotta wait and read about it in the monthly newsletter?"

He should have known better, he thought. Wolf grapevine was worse than YouTube when it came to news.

Chapter Twenty-Five

Preparing and cooking breakfast for sixteen hungry werewolves was hard work, Airic thought. Sheesh, why she wanted to make biscuits was beyond her. Martha had been stupefied when she'd asked permission to work beside her. She thought about that as she cut more of the batter into circles.

"I know how to make pretty good biscuits. May I do that, please?" Seemed a reasonable question to her, but the kitchen had done one of those noisy silence things again. Martha, the cook, had looked shocked.

"You are mistress here, and you may do anything you like. This kitchen is yours to command."

Airic looked around the room and realized that they were waiting for her to get pissy with the woman. Why, she didn't know, but it seemed a turning point to the morning. "I am only mistress in the studio where I work. I have everything in its place. Everything is where I want it, just how I want it. That is my domain, not here. Would you come in and start throwing a pot or paint just because you've done it at home before? No, you'd ask me first, wouldn't you? This is your area of expertise, Miss Martha.

I'm the novice here. And as such, I ask your permission to use your things in your kitchen." After her nod of approval, Airic set to work. She had also made the tea.

That was another weird stepping point. Mrs. Wolff had asked her if she'd like a glass of iced tea, that she had made a fresh pitcher just today, and when she had said yes, several people had rolled their eyes. When she had taken her first sip, thank God it was only a sip, she gagged.

"Wow, that's sweet! I can't possibly drink that; I don't know how anyone could." With tears in her eyes, she noticed that it was just her and Mrs. Wolff in the room. Shit! They had cleared out fast!

"Yes, it is incredibly sweet, isn't it? I've been trying for years, and I mean years, to find someone brave enough who would tell me that. I kept making it sweeter and sweeter thinking someone would say, 'hey, this is awful.' I hate making it. I hate drinking it. Thank you." She sat down at the table and started peeling potatoes again.

"Well why didn't you just tell someone that instead of trying to put them into a sugar coma?" Airic dumped the whole pitcher in the sink and put water on to boil. While that was working, she found the tea bags and counted out what she needed. No sugar, not in her tea. It was always easier to add more than to take away she thought.

"But this was so much more fun. You should see the ways they've come up with to dump it. Most of the time it was in that big plant by the dining room, or over the railing when they thought I wasn't looking. The poor plant had to be transplanted last fall because there was something wrong with the soil, the lady said. Too much sugar byproducts, I would guess."

Airic couldn't help it. She leaned over and kissed the woman on her cheek and laughed. One by one, the women returned to the kitchen to resume work.

Airic was still smiling when she felt him. Bradley. He was coming home, err here, she thought. She looked behind her because it had felt as if he had run his fingers down her spine. Closing her eyes, she saw him, running. He was a wolf and coming with the others. When she opened her eyes, Donna was smiling at her.

"Neat, huh? The first time I felt David it damn near made me jump off the ladder I was on. Do you know how long?"

"Maybe thirty minutes…how did you know? I mean, I've never…" Airic cut out the last biscuit in the last batch and went to the oven. She was embarrassed and frustrated. He shouldn't be doing these things to her, she was leaving soon.

"You're his mate; you'll always be able to feel him. Especially when he wants you specifically to know he's coming." With a pat on her shoulder, Donna waddled away.

What the hell was that supposed to mean? But she didn't have time to ask. Donna announced that the alpha and men were thirty minutes away and to hop to it.

The kitchen became an artist palate of smells and sounds to her. From the ham and beef cooking, sizzling in the pans, the eggs cracked on the side of the bowl for omelets to the coffee being brewed in the giant urn on the counter. Each woman knew her job and the small sounds of ice tinkling in the glasses to the juicer squeezing oranges, the air perfumed with their sweetness, all came together as a musical telling of love and respect for each other. Airic wished again for her sketch pad and a few minutes to capture the room, but she'd have to wait until she got home to put it to paper.

***

By the time they were less than hundred yards from the house, they could smell the food. Each wolf stopped and sniffed the air; meat, and the sweet smell of other foods cooking scented the very air around them. They took off much faster then, running and romping to the house. Several of the younger wolves nipped at the older ones' tails and ran when they gave chase. Tumbling and jumping, he thought one would never know what a grizzly discovery they had just made. This is what they needed and he'd have to make sure his grandmother knew how much he appreciated it.

As each wolf shifted, they went to the outdoor showers to clean up and dress. His wolves weren't very modest, and being naked most of the time didn't bother them at all, but Bradley had made sure they all knew that there was a stranger in the house and to behave. He hoped that she was up; he wanted them all to meet her.

He felt her the moment he walked into the house. His body hardened in response to her scent. He needed to find her, to touch her. He followed her scent into the kitchen and was almost bowled over by two women coming out with platters of food. He saw her across the room and strode toward her, unmindful of the chaos he was creating in his wake. The master just didn't come into the kitchen at meal times.

He watched her hand the bowl of food to the woman standing next to her and come toward him, never breaking eye contact with him. When he reached her, he pulled her into his arms and kissed her, devoured her, tasted her. Both of them forgot about the room full of people and the dining room full of more.

He pulled her tight against him, loving the feel of her warmth and strength. She opened her mouth beneath his and he swept his tongue inside her sweet heat, tasting the honey she'd just eaten. When he felt the tug at his arm, he slapped out at it. When it continued to pull and yank, he turned to snarl at the nuisance. Grandda.

"Go away. I'm busy." He growled at the older man. And was turning back to kiss her again when he felt him pull again. "I mean it, old man, go away."

"Bradley, my boy, you need to let the little girl go so she can feed the others too. If you stay in this kitchen kissing her, then the rest of the food won't get served." Bradley looked at the now vacant kitchen with all the serving platters and bowls just sitting ready to be taken in the other room. With a sigh of regret, he let her go, but not without another quick kiss and a promised "later" did he walk away, grabbing a platter and taking it with him.

Chapter Twenty-Six

There were sixteen wolves and two vampires at the table that morning. The one vamp Airic had met and she tried to ignore him. Aaron, he had told her, was the man from her house. The other was a big man too, and just as gorgeous as the others. Bradley had called him Dominic; he was a tracker.

The breakfast had been a good idea, the men were starved. It got a little dicey there for a few minutes when she began pouring tea in everyone's glasses. She hadn't asked if they wanted it, just poured. When two of them looked around for the potted plant that she'd had moved outside to the deck in deference to the large crowd, she nearly laughed out loud. Bradley looked panicky and nervous, especially when his grams, as he called her, told him she was trying a different way to brew the tea, and she wanted him to taste it for her. He cautiously put the glass to his lips and pretended to take a drink.

"Oh come on now, take a healthy drink. I need to know if I should add more sugar or not." She watched in amazement as he put the brew to his mouth and took a big swallow. The look on his face was priceless. He had expected it to be so sweet, as she had always brewed it, but was surprised by no sugar at all.

"Hey, hey, this is really good. Really, really good." She watched as he realized what he had said and his face flamed red. His grams took pity on him and kissed his cheek and told him that Airic had made it, and she was handing the tea brewing over to her in the future.

After all the food was eaten and the plates cleared away, Bradley asked to speak to her. She told him she was drying dishes, but if he wanted to come in and help, she'd get it done a lot faster. She didn't think he would, but he followed her in the kitchen and took a towel out of the drawer. After the others realized he wasn't kidding and he was going to help, clean up began.

"Grams, thanks so much for getting this done. I didn't realize how hungry everyone was until we smelled the food coming across the field." He was drying one of the large plates that wouldn't fit in one of the two dishwashers.

"I didn't do it, Airic did. She said you guys would want a fine meal and told us what to do."

Airic glared at her. All she had said was they'd be hungry. *Fine meal indeed,* she thought with a huff.

"You did this, all of this?"

She looked at his shocked expression and got even madder. "You know, I can think beyond the wheel, you moronic ass. And that's another thing. I'd like for someone to take me home. Today." She had just finished drying the last pot and hung the towel over the oven door like her mother had always done.

"I can take you; you must be running out of clothes. I should have thought of that. But my shirt on you looks mighty delicious. I can't wait to take it off you, button by button, inch by inch. Tasting you as I go." He had moved closer once he had set his towel aside, his voice getting deeper and warmer. Her body responded to it, nipples hardening, breasts tightening. Need, she felt his need for her touch her in very intimate and seductive ways.

"No, not you. You...you must be tired. I can have one...don't do that, Bradley." He was touching her again. She could not think when he touched her. "Please, you have to..."

"Yes, I do. I have to very badly, love. I want you, Alastriona. I need to bury myself deep inside of you." His mouth moved along her jaw and to her ear. He nipped at her lobe and she felt the room tilt. He moved his hands up her ribs and cupped her bare breasts, his thumbs finding her nipples and caressing them. He moaned deep from his chest. It vibrated along her skin like a caress. She noticed that they were alone again. Everyone had cleared out without a sound.

"Unbutton your shirt. Unbutton it for me." With shaky fingers, she moved to do what he asked. When it was undone, she looked at him and closed her eyes when she felt the cool breeze touch her. "Look at me, Alastriona; I want you to watch me as I take you into my mouth." She opened her eyes again and he lifted her up off the floor, lifting her by her ass and along his body to have her wrap her legs around his waist. When her breasts were level with his mouth, she opened the shirt and cupping her own breasts, fed him them.

"Oh Bradley, yes!" She watched as he suckled at one breast then the other, nipping harder and harder with each pass of his mouth. She was rocking into him now; her release was close, so close she could almost taste it.

"I want you, to be inside of you. Now, Alastriona, now." While she tightened her legs around him, she felt him move to his pants. The zipper moving down, each tooth opened was like a sensual stroke along her clit. Running her fingers through his hair and gripping it tightly between her fingers, she pulled his mouth up and to hers. Her tongue invaded his mouth, taking and dueling with his, tasting his heat, his need.

"Please, hurry, please." She was begging, begging him to complete her, fill her. Her body wasn't just on fire; it felt like molten lava was running through her veins.

This time it was she who heard the person at the door, she who snarled at him to go the fuck away.

"You really need to come out here, my lord. There is a man here who says he's here because of a rogue wolf that they have tracked to our territory. I thought it could be the one from yesterday." The man on the other side of the door sounded terrified. He fucking well should be, she thought.

Her body hurt, ached like it never had before. Bradley was still holding her, his pants not quite all the way open, and she wondered if he felt the same way. When he didn't answer the man, she heard him clear his throat again and she answered for the alpha.

"Tell him that he'll be right there, please. Put him in the small room off the front door, the one with the pretty blue vase on the table." She leaned her head back against the cabinet behind her when he sat her down on it.

"Small salon, Samuel, put him in the small salon as the mistress said." He was still looking at her hungrily as he pulled the tab back up on his trousers and redid his belt. With that look, she started panting again. "You keep looking at me like that, love, and that man could good and well rot away in there for all I care."

"I hope he does rot. Fucking dick head." She didn't get down, but watched him get dressed and straighten his clothes. He was grinning now, the arrogant ass.

"We are going to have to find a place where no one knows where we are. Then I'm going to fuck your brains out. Then when I'm finished, I'm going to do it again. Then maybe a couple more times for good measure." He placed both hands on either side of her, trapping her where she was. As if she needed to be trapped, she thought. He kissed her. Pulling away much too soon for her, he pulled her shirt closed, picked her up, and stood her on the floor. With a stern, "get dressed," and a hard swat on the ass, he left the room.

Tossing another "arrogant asshole" his way, she went to the laundry room. She knew he heard her, because she heard him laugh as he went.

Chapter Twenty-Seven

He stared at the man across from him. Donna had brought in iced tea for each of the three men, the man who said his name was Peter Alastair, Dom who was acting bodyguard for Bradley, and himself. The story he had told them did not set well with Bradley.

"We have come into your territory without notice, sire. And I want to extend my master's apologies. We have tracked a rogue male into this region who we believe to be dangerous and quite mad. He has killed before, humans and weres alike without discrimination, and had now gotten the taste of human blood. We will destroy him as is our way." Peter recited this speech. Recited it because, Bradley thought, he'd done this many times before.

"Where do you think this rogue wolf is, and why come into my territory?" The man wasn't lying, not really. He did believe the wolf to be dangerous and maybe even mad, but not about him being destroyed.

"We have tracked him a short distance from here, in small region just north of the city. About seventy miles, I think. We believe that he may be holing up in a house there with a woman. The woman maybe a part of this or not, we cannot say." The man took a gulp of the tea and set it on the table next to Alastriona's pretty blue vase. Alastriona lived about seventy miles due north of here.

"This region, do you have an address of the female helping him? I'll send you help and get this taken care of very quickly. I don't want a rogue in my territory any longer than necessary." Bradley watched the man stiffen.

"Oh no! I mean, no, that'll be all right. We will...can. We can take care of him, the male. It's a rogue male, I believe I mentioned. They can be quite mad, and dangerous, as you may already know. My master has said that while we appreciate you wanting to help, he would rather take care of this on our own."

"I see. The address then. I wouldn't want my men to stumble into your trouble then. Donna, would you please ask your mistress to meet me in the barn, please? Dom, go with her." Bradley had put just enough command in his voice to have his wolves obey without question, even to the point of leaving the alpha alone with this man. The other man, Peter, didn't feel a thing, which Bradley found to be curious, but he would think on that later. For now, he didn't like this, any of this.

After securing the address and giving him the assurances that they would be close if they needed any extra help, Peter left.

Putting out a mental call, Bradley had three of his wolves track the man in the limo. As soon as he left the estate, Bradley would know where he was at every second. He strode to the barn and to his mate. Moving with quick strides, he pulled out his cell phone and made three calls. The first was to his brother David, the cop.

"David, a man just left here saying that he had a rogue were on the loose close to here. Said he was dangerous and that he is living with a female helper in this territory." He saw her then, leaning against the fence, petting his favorite ride.

"Do you think it was the were that killed last night?" He could hear David shutting the door to his office as he spoke.

"No, I think he's lying. The address this man gave me, he claims this male is hiding out in is Alastriona's. I think it's either the man from the phone call, or he's his flunky and they're here to take her back with them. That isn't going to happen, David. She's mine, Alastriona is mine." Bradley saw that Dom was scanning the area, watching. Good, he understood that he had wanted him to protect her. It was several seconds before he realized that his brother hadn't said anything.

"David, what is it?"

"When I got back to the house this morning, Donna told me that Airic, what she told them to call her by the way, had made her sit down and rest her feet as soon as she came downstairs. She apparently came down just after we left this morning. She'd even gone so far as to get a bucket of cold water for her to help with the swelling of her ankles. It seems that throughout the morning she had made all the breeding women go out to the poolside and drink a glass of juice and rest ten minutes out of every hour. Not asked, but commanded, Bradley, while she, your alpha, made biscuits and brewed tea with them and worked beside them. Donna said that when Phil and Daniel came in, the two pups from last week, she asked them to help out Martha and weed the garden and she'd pay them for their troubles. She gave each of them twenty bucks apiece and several of the first batch of her biscuits with honey on them. Since I've been in my office, I've had twenty-three phone calls asking if the rumors were true, that the alpha has yet to claim his alpha queen. Bradley, have you? Claimed her, I mean."

His alpha queen, not bitch but queen. That was the highest honor given to a pack bitch. It wasn't something that you claimed as yours, but was given to you by your people. Alastriona had been with the pack for just over twenty-four hours and she was their queen.

"I need you to watch things for me until tomorrow. I'm going to call Grandda and Aaron too. If you need me, and you had better really need me, your queen and I will be at the cabin." He heard David laughing as he hung up. He called his grandda next, telling him that he was going to be out of touch until tomorrow, and asked if he could keep an eye on things.

"You gonna claim that girl? Heard tell they've made her their queen. 'Bout time if'n you ask me. Breed that one quick, boy. I ain't getting any younger."

With a very heartfelt "fuck off," Bradley hung up on him. He called Aaron next and told him the same thing. But Aaron had news for him too.

"Pete just called, she's got a name for the phone you gave her. A Christopher Alastair is the owner of the number that called the phone delivered to Airic. He's an alpha from Europe, or so the address says. She got with Bailey and she was able to run down some other interesting information. It seems there are several unsolved deaths that may or may not be connected to him. Over the past several years, hummm, eight years, there have been nine women whom he claimed as his mates that were found brutally raped and beaten to death a few months later. There are eleven other women still missing in that region. I've contacted the master vampire of that realm and he said that there have been several of his female vamps raped as well, but they can't give a description of the man, or sometimes men, who did it. But he did say that a male wolf was involved. Not alpha, but a male wolf."

"This Christopher, does he have a brother named Peter by any chance?" Bradley started toward Alastriona again, his fear for her safety paramount.

"Yeah, and one named Slavic. Slavic was one of the ones Bailey took out two years ago when she was hired by Mel to find them. He was the leader of the six she tracked to Airic's cave. Maybe he wasn't the leader, but this Christopher was, you think?" Bradley had always liked Aaron's quick mind. They could and had worked out issues together any number of times since becoming friends. He needed him now.

"I was going to the cabin in the woods on the estate. I was going there to be alone with Alastriona, but now I'm not so sure that's a good idea. I don't suppose you'd put us up for the night and leave us the fuck alone, would you? Aaron, I've been trying for three days to claim my mate and there have been any number of crises occurring to prevent that. I need to claim her now, before this jackass tries to take her from me."

"I'm sorry, buddy, but if the only reason you're claiming her is because you don't want this guy to take her from you, then no. Sara'd have my nuts in a jar so quick I wouldn't know they were missing until it was too late. But for love, ah, that I can do."

As soon as this was over, he was going to make a list of those who he was going to kill first, and the deaths would be very slow, long and slow. Aaron was working his way to the top, right after his grandda, he thought

"I love her, you prick, and you damn well know it. We'll be there in fifteen minutes. Less if I can get her to shift with me." He hung up on him as well.

Now, he had to tell Alastriona what they were going to do and hoped that his nuts weren't in the jar next to Aaron's.

Chapter Twenty-Eight

She watched him come across the field then stop to talk on the phone. She wasn't naive enough to think that Donna had really sent her and Dom out here to check to see if the horses were fed. The urgency in her voice had made her do it without question. Then there was the fact that she could see the gun that Dom was carrying under his shirt and then the way he kept looking around every ten seconds.

The horses were beautiful. There were at least a dozen in the paddock here and Dom had said that there were at least a dozen more that ran free on the compound. She wished she could ride, but she'd never been on one before and was a little afraid of the huge beast.

"Mistress, we need to go into the barn now. Please?" Dom was looking to the field just behind her and she didn't hesitate but let him lead her there. There was a huge gray wolf sitting near the middle of the barn when they entered. She stopped walking and Dom walked into her.

"He won't hurt you; he's a friend of the pack. His name is Tristan. His mate, Bailey, is coming as well. You need to move closer to him and touch his fur before he'll shift back." Dom didn't move any closer to the wolf either, but stood at her side, his hand now on the butt of the gun.

"Why? Why is he here? Why do I have to touch him, and why is Bailey coming soon? What's happening, Dom? And where is Bradley?" She was suddenly very afraid. This was more than the man in the small salon, this was much more.

"Touch the wolf, please, mistress. He cannot understand us when he is in this form. He isn't a true wolf, but a vampire who can shift. Bailey is coming because she is needed, and Alpha is coming now. You must trust me, I would die for you." Dom dropped to his knees and rubbed his neck along her leg. She was so going to have to find out what that meant and why they kept doing it to her and only her.

Airic walked slowly over to the wolf and reached out to touch him. But a stirring in the air stopped her. A falcon, a beautiful pedigree falcon, swooped into the barn and landed not five feet from the wolf. As she stared at the bird, it shimmered and shifted into a woman. Airic took a step back. There was something familiar about the woman and she didn't like it.

"Hello, Ms. Bennett, it's Bailey. Remember me? I found you in the cave. Please touch my mate. I can tell him to shift, but he can smell your fear and doesn't want to frighten you more than he already has."

"Yes, I remember you now, and despite my telling you to leave me there, you brought me out anyway. Why should I do anything for you because you ask me to?" Glaring at the woman, she moved forward again.

Her heart started to race hard within her chest. Then as quickly as it started, she realized Bradley was there and she slowed hers, and knew that somehow, she had calmed his as well. That was just freaky, she thought.

"You're all scaring her. Stop it now! Bailey, please move back, all right?" Bradley. And he was pissed, if his voice was any indication.

"Mistress, touch the wolf. He wants only to help you," Dom was saying.

"Ms. Bennett, we were asked to come here to protect you." Bailey too was talking.

It was suddenly too much. She couldn't take it one second more and turned to Bradley. "I am not scared! I'm pissed off. All of you shut up." Turning to the wolf, she pointed and shouted, "You! Shift! Now!" And just like that, the wolf was a man.

She jerked her hand behind her and backed toward where Bradley was. She had done that. She had welded the energy, had felt it run down her arm and then through her finger and into the man. And she had hurt him.

Running to him, she could hear his moans. She knew what it was to shift and it was painful and hard. She couldn't image what it would be like to shift in a second. But he had.

"I'm so sorry. I'm so sorry. I'm so sorry. Here, let me help you up. I didn't know…please tell me you're all right." She was searching him, looking for any indication that she had caused him more than the usual pain.

"Damn, lady, remind me to never piss you off," the vampire exclaimed.

Airic burst into tears. It was just too much too fast. She heard them talking but paid little attention until

Bradley asked her to please release Dom. She looked over at Dom and was startled for a few seconds.

He had his gun out and pointed at the vampire's head and his arm gripped around his throat. His eyes were golden and his canines were extended.

"Baby, Dom was told to protect you at all costs. He thinks that Tristan has hurt you and that's why you're crying. Tell him to release him, tell him you're fine, or they'll both die."

She looked back at Bradley. His voice was calm, but his heart was pounding again. She could feel it in her own chest.

"I don't understand. I can feel your heart. I don't understand any of this. Why would they both die? No one hurt me." Her head hurt, she realized. An ache like she'd never had before.

"Because if he pulls that trigger and kills my mate, I will fucking rip him apart, that's how they'll both die. Release him or I fucking will." Bailey was standing behind Dom shaking with barely suppressed anger. Airic could feel her strength radiating out of her.

"Bailey, you aren't helping the matter. Honey, look at me. I'll explain everything, but right now, you need to tell Dom to let Tristan go." He was stroking her, soothing her.

Airic nodded and stood up. She swayed slightly, but after a few seconds, the dizziness went away. She walked over to the two men and touched her wolf. Hers, Dom was hers. She knew that what he had said earlier was true. He would die for her.

"Dom, release him. I'm okay. Please let him go and put your gun away. Thank you. You have no idea what it's like to have a stranger want to protect me so fully. Let him go, now please." She watched as he pulled his gun away from the man and let go of his neck. Dom stepped back two steps and dropped again to the ground.

This neck rubbing, or whatever it was called, was different this time. After he had touched his neck to her leg, he rolled over to his back and laid there. Instinctually, she knew what he wanted. Leaning down, she rubbed his belly and then his throat. He growled gently at the back of his throat.

Chapter Twenty-Nine

Airic was riding in front of Bradley on his horse with his one arm gripped tightly around her waist and they were tearing across the field as fast as he could take them. She looked up in the sky and watched Bailey fly over them with her mate Tristan just behind her. She thought they looked like they were playing tag. Looking down, she watched as wolves ran alongside of them, racing and jumping over every obstacle in their path without seemingly seeing them.

Bradley had said he would explain, but there wasn't time now. He needed to get her to safety then they would talk. Her head was pounding, like a sludge hammer was beating its way into her skull. She leaned back into his embrace.

"Baby, I'm having a hard time watching the path with your breasts bobbing up and down like that." His voice was low and very close to her ear. He nuzzled her neck and desire shot though her instantly.

She realized that she could feel his hard cock pressing into her back. Reaching behind her, she ran her hand down the hard shaft and felt him lengthen beneath her hand.

"Bradley."

He pulled her closer and moved his fingers in the button gap on her shirt just below her breast. He cupped her and with his thumb and forefinger, pinched her nipple, then tugged at it. "I want you, right now. If there weren't so many people around, and your safety wasn't a problem, I'd stop this horse right now, strip you naked, and take you right here. Then I'd ride as hard as I could with you bouncing up and down on my cock. Christ, I want to fuck you." Closing her eyes, she could see them doing just that and pressed harder against his cock with her hand. He growled at her.

They teased and played with each other all the way to Aaron's estate. By the time they got there, she was so hot she felt as if she would combust if Bradley touched her right now and maybe even if he didn't.

Once they were in the mansion, they were ushered to a big room by a dapper-looking man who said his name was Duncan. He offered them something to eat and drink and they declined both. Carrying a large silver tray that somehow seemed to be a part of his uniform, though why she thought that she had no idea, he took them to see the master.

"Ms. Bennett. How lovely for you to join us. It's nice to see you again." Aaron came forward and kissed her hand.

"You! You're that vampire that…where is she? That woman who knock me out." Airic turned when she saw him look over his shoulder.

"Hello, dear. Welcome to my home. I know you're angry right now, but we need to focus on the issue at hand." She patted the seat next to her.

Airic sat in the chair closest to the door. She was being spiteful, she knew, but damn it, she'd like to have one thing go right today. "Bradley, what is she talking about? What issue?" Bradley didn't answer, but simply picked her up and sat down in her chair with her on his lap. Okay, she thought, this is much better.

"I'm afraid that since we talked last, there has been another development. Your friend Diana Lake has gone missing, as you know. It seems that Christopher Alastair, the master wolf that had you turned, has taken her and will return her only for you, my dear." Airic looked at Bradley after Aaron made his announcement. He knew this, she thought, and he'd known this since before they left his home.

Chapter Thirty

He knew the moment she figured it out. Her body became stiff and she sat up. He'd thought to tell her about Diana as soon as they got on the horse, but he got distracted just as he said. Now it was too late. She'd think that he had played with her because he didn't want to tell her. Okay, well that was true, but not all of it. Damn it, she had touched him first.

When she rose off his lap, he pulled her back down. She was not getting away until he had time to explain. And she was going to listen to him. He was the alpha, damn it.

"Sit still and listen to me, damn it. You're not going anywhere half-cocked," he shouted. He hated yelling, but…

When he felt the cold water hit his face, he opened his eyes. *What the fuck?* He was lying flat on the floor. No not on the floor, he decided, but on the chair, which was on the floor, his legs still hanging off the seat, which was now in the air.

"Welcome back." Aaron, smiling, was holding a large bucket that was dripping water on his chest. He had poured water on him. He didn't remember a thing after pulling Airic back down onto his lap.

"What...why did you do that?" He had missed something. He wasn't sure what, but something was... "Airic! Where's Airic?" He started scrambling to get up when Aaron's booted foot slammed him back down in the chair.

"If you sit up now, you might start the bleeding again and I just got it to stop. Airic is upstairs in the pink bedroom with Sara and Lizzy. I'd leave her there for the moment if I were you. She hit you with Duncan's tray and opened your empty head with it." Setting down the empty bucket, Aaron pulled another chair over and sat down next to him.

"Can I at least ask why she hit me? Or do you, in your all-knowing wisdom, not know why?" He glared at him as Aaron grinned down to him, cocky bastard. "He's just made it to the top of my 'To Kill' list," he muttered to himself.

"Oh she told us. Quite loudly, as a matter of fact, and several times since you hit the floor. It was very enjoyable to me, I must say, to see someone else I know make a woman that mad that quickly. Let's see if I can remember it all...you're an arrogant asshole, which I must say, we all knew that one. Hummm, let's see, you will not manhandle her and get away with it, which I'm pretty sure you did not by the looks of that gash. You will not keep secrets from her, that one was a surprise to me. I didn't think you could keep secrets from each other once you bonded. Oh yeah, she was questioning your parental background and was quite sure you had some snake in your DNA. I'm sure that I missed a couple, I was kind of busy trying to get the tray from her before she cold-cocked you again." He leaned back after delivering his speech. Bradley wanted to get up and pound his ass, but his head hurt now, he realized.

"We aren't bonded, not yet anyway, and you know it. That's why we were coming here, remember? Shit, that fucking hurts." He had reached up and tenderly touched the area. His fingers came away with blood on them. Damn woman. He grinned suddenly.

"Oh, I don't like that. That cannot be a good sign." Aaron grinned back with him. Bradley put out his hand and Aaron pulled him and the chair to an upright position. "So, going to use the guilt thing, huh? Could work, but only if you hurry. You seem to be healing already." Bradley saluted him and took off. He did warn him that they weren't to be disturbed unless the house was on fire and only then if they were the next room about to go up in flames.

He didn't knock, but walked in. Sara was standing at the bathroom door and Lizzy was pouting on the bed. He winked at her.

"I'm very mad at you, Uncle Bradley. You said you'd wait for me to grow up and we'd get married someday." She was the cutest six-year-old little girl he knew. She was also the only six-year-old little girl he knew.

"Sorry, love, but things happen. Besides, I'd be an old man by the time you wanted to get married, and you wouldn't want me then." His heart melted when she puckered out her lower lip at him.

"What on earth makes you think you have a snowball's chance in hell of living long enough to get old?" Alastriona, his mate.

155

He grinned again and motioned for Sara, who was barely upright she was laughing so hard, and Lizzy to leave them alone. He thumbed the lock on the bedroom door. "Come out of there, Alastriona, we are going to talk." He tried to sound stern and hard, but he was pretty sure she'd hear the humor creeping in.

The door slammed open. Yeah, she'd heard it. He smiled at the sight she made. Her hair had come down at some point on the ride over and it flowed down her back and over her left shoulder. Her eyes, normally a deep shade of chocolate brown, were glowing golden in her anger. Her breasts, unfettered by a bra, were heaving and tight against her shirt. *Mine.* He had thought that before, but now, right now, she was his. He moved to her, unbuttoning his shirt as he walked.

"What the fuck do you think you're doing?" She backed up two steps and looked around.

Mine, he thought again and again. "If you go into that bathroom again and shut the door, I'm going to break it down. And that will only piss me off. Take off your clothes, Alastriona, or I'll do it for you." He tossed his shirt toward the chair by the fireplace.

"I'm not taking anything off and you aren't either. Stop that, Bradley, this has gone far enough."

He slid his belt from his trousers and threw it in the same general direction. "No it hasn't. We've almost gotten there a few times, but no, we haven't gone near far enough, but we will. Take. Off. Your. Clothes, Alastriona." He could almost touch her now and he could smell her. She was aroused. Very aroused, if her scent was any indication.

"You...you hurt me. And lied to me. Why? Why, Bradley? I...don't touch me, I'm trying to...Bradley, you...you have to stop that." Her moan nearly had his knees buckling when he touched her cheek.

"I want you, love. Come to me. Come and let me make love with you, Alastriona." He gently ran his knuckles over her nipples that were poking tight against the shirt. She bowed into his touch.

Bradley pulled her to him a slow step at a time. She resisted it, but not very hard. When he had her just inches away, he began undoing the buttons for her. She watched him work the tiny little buttons through the equally tiny holes. Or had his fingers just grown too large for such a simple task?

When he got them all undone, he lifted her chin up so that he could look her in the eye. Not touching any other part of her body, he pushed the shirt off her shoulders and let if fall to the floor. Neither of them seemed to notice.

Her eyes were golden and sharp. His need for her, all of her, was reflected back to him from them.

He unsnapped his own pants, pulled the tab down to the bottom, and then let them fall to the floor with her shirt. He put his thumbs into his boxer briefs and pushed them down over his hips, and then he leaned down and pulled them off. Dropping to his knees before her, he placed his hands on her hips, over the pair of his boxers she had put on this morning.

"I want to make love to you, baby." He didn't move, didn't breathe for fear she'd turn him down.

"Yes, please, Bradley. Please."

Chapter Thirty-One

Slowly, he pulled the pants down her hips. He kissed her skin as he revealed it. She tasted delicious, he thought.

He lifted her leg and pulled the pants off, then did the same to the other leg. Sitting back on his feet, he looked at the wonder before him. *Mine.*

"You are beautiful, the most beautiful creature I have ever seen. And you're mine. All mine. I thought that I was in love before, but I wasn't. This, this that I feel for you right now is love. I love you, Alastriona. I love you with all that I am." He stood up, leaned over, picked her up, cradled her in his arms, and carried her to the big bed. Gently, he laid her down and stood over her, between her legs, and just looked at her.

"Bradley, I...I've never been in love before, had never thought to after the accident, but I do love you. You irritate me to distraction most times, but I love you." She reached up for him and he knelt before her.

Lifting her legs, he placed them on his shoulders. It was then that he noticed the tattoo encircling her left thigh. It was his pack's tribal, a duplicate of the one worn around his own bicep, the one his grandda had put there when he had reached manhood. He touched it reverently and looked up at her. She was watching him.

"Where did you get this, love?" He ran his finger around it again, feeling her shudder in response. He was not at all surprised to feel her response move along his tattoo as well.

"I don't know. I've never seen it before...please, touch it again." She was breathless and when he touched it, she moaned. "Bradley, please...I need, I need you to bond with me. Now, right now." Her urgency pushed him forward. He licked her nether lips and tasted her cream. Her whimpering became begging.

Standing up, he moved up on the bed, taking her with him so that she was beneath him. With is cock positioned at her core, he lifted her chin to look at him.

"I don't want to hurt you, baby, but I can't wait. I need...holy Christ!" She took him into her, not far enough to break through her virginity, but enough to set him on fire. He surged forward hard and fast. And made her his. *Mine, she's finally mine,* he thought.

Tight, she was so fucking tight around him. He didn't move for a full minute even though it felt like an eternity. He wanted to pound into her again and again, but he waited. He looked down at her and grinned at her expression.

"What's the matter, are we done already? That didn't seem all the much fun after all that build up at my house and this morning. I'm sorely disappointed, because I gotta tell you, Bradley, you aren't very good at this. At least not as good as I thought you'd be anyway."

He burst out laughing. She had to hurt, he knew he was larger than most men, and she was making jokes. At least he hoped it was a joke. He slid his hand down along her hip, pulled her leg up over his, and rocked gently into her.

"Maybe I could improve a little if I had some help. Men don't like to do all the work themselves, you know." He rocked again, harder this time. His eyes nearly rolled to the back of his head when she tilted her hips up to take more of him into her.

"I want to be on top of you. Oh, Bradley…I'll…I'll show you how it's done then. Women like to do all the work. I…oh my…" He rolled over onto his back, taking her with him. He placed his hands on her hips and showed her how to move over him, ride him. She was a very fast learner.

"Cup your breasts for me. I want you to touch yourself, make your nipples pink for me." He watched as she ran her palms across her nipples, moaning as she did. He couldn't help it, he surged hard into her.

"Do you like this? Is this what you want? I love it when you suck on my nipples. It makes me wet. The harder you suckle at them, the wetter I get."

His cock seemed to have a mind of its own, he thought. He sat up and wrapped his hands around her waist, pulled her up, and slammed her down onto him. "Feed me. Feed me those succulent nipples." His mouth covered her offerings and he sucked hard, pulling it into his mouth and nipping at the bud. She screamed. Her climax rocketed thorough her and straight into him. Flipping her to her back, he slammed his release into her, filling her with his cum, his seed. Over and over he exploded into her, even after her hands fell limply at her sides, he came. When he finally emptied himself into her, only then did he collapse on top of her. He didn't think he'd ever be able to move again. Well, at least for the next five minutes, he mused.

"Baby, I need to make you mine, mine so that everyone will know you belong to me. I wanted to explain before, but we got...sidetracked. I need to mark you. I need to bite you. All right?" She stiffened slightly. He knew what he was asking her would be hard, especially after what she had experienced in the cave to be changed.

"I...will I need to...I've never bit anyone before. Well, that's not true. I bit Jamie Grove in first grade, but he had tried to kiss me. His lips looked like a bullfrog all puffed out like that. But I don't think this is gonna be the same, is it?"

God, he loved her. "No, not the same. You don't need to bite me tonight, but yes, you will need to eventually. The sooner the better, actually. You need to draw blood, and keep your canines in my skin for a little while. Your essences will flow into me, marking me as yours too. Have you...stop moving like that. Christ, woman...have you ever dropped just your canines before?" He rocked into her as she had moved against him. He was hard again and getting harder by the second. And if she kept moving like that, he'd be coming again too. Not that that sounded so bad.

"Yes, oh yes, harder. Canines? Oh no, I've never...Oh, Bradley, that's it, harder, please. I can't think when you...draw blood; if you stop again, I will draw blood, but not nicely. Canines in the flesh. Oh my, oh please, Bradley, more."

He was teasing her, he knew, but he couldn't help it. He loved hearing her confused and flustered. He rocked again, this time with meaning, and kissed her. He wanted to make love with her slowly this time, but as soon as she wrapped her legs around his hips and locked them at his back, he was lost. In no time at all, she was coming, her climax pushing him into his own. Roaring out his own fulfillment, he once again dropped on top of her. But he quickly moved to his side, and then on to his back, taking her with him.

Moving his mouth to her shoulder, he nuzzled the area and she tilted her head to the side, giving him the extra room he needed to bite. Licking the area to take away most of the pain, he bit her, hard and fast. Her blood filled his mouth, hot and spicy. He didn't move when he felt her hand touch the same area on his own shoulder, moving his hair to the side. Raising her head up just a little, she licked him and sank her teeth deep into his flesh. As soon as his blood touched her tongue and she swallowed, he felt the unbreakable connection between them. *Mine. She is truly mine.*

Chapter Thirty-Two

It was hours later when they were lying across from each other in the huge bathtub filled with hot water that he remembered the painting from the first day. They had slept for a few hours, woke, and made love again before Bradley thought a nice hot soak would do them both a world of good.

"There was a painting of a blue house that you sent to the gallery; do you remember where you got the idea to paint it?" He picked up her foot and began massaging it, starting at her toes and working his way up her calf.

"The one with the little boys painting it? Yes, I remember it. It was a dream I had while I was still in the hospital. There were these two little boys and they wanted to get back at someone, I'm not sure who, could have been the people in the house. Anyway, the older one had gotten the paint. He had gone to several hardware stores and department stores getting what they needed without raising suspicion. The younger one had done reconnaissance work for days, I guess. I seem to remember he had a chart with times on it. I remember thinking when I woke up what a resourceful couple of kids they were. Then so they wouldn't get caught, they stripped down to their bare butts and painted the whole house, windows included, that lovely shade of blue. I think its called robin's egg. I loved painting that picture; I think I laughed for the first time in months when I did it here recently. Why do you ask?" She had been playing with the oversized sponge while she told him the story, and looked up at him when she was finished.

He could only stare at her. That was exactly how they'd done it. Over a two week time frame, he had gone to different stores all over the county buying what they could afford that day. He bet if he looked around, he could probably find David's notebook and the chart he had made calculating the time they needed versus the time the Morgans were gone. Then he thought, she had said it had made her laugh, laugh for the first time in months. Fate, or the Fates, had made her his, and gave her one of his fond memories to make her laugh.

"Bradley? Why did you ask about that particular painting?"

With a huge smile and a lighter heart, and after swearing her to secrecy of course, he told her of two wolves getting back at Mr. Morgan for telling their dad how he had caught them necking with the Ashley twins in his hay barn.

"Necking, huh? Maybe that's why you aren't very good at this sex thing." He watched as she slithered toward him, her bottom just above the water line.

"Sex thing? Alastriona, that was not a sex thing, that was the real thing. We should talk about the claiming ceremony. The full moon is in two days." She moved up his body and over his legs. When he reached out to touch her, she placed his hands on the side of the tub.

"Hummm, I thought you already claimed me. It certainly felt like it anyway. The way you slid inside of me, deep and hard. And your bite along my neck, your teeth in my skin, hummm, makes me want you again." Her voice got huskier and deeper as she spoke. She was sitting astride his thighs, not near close enough for him, he thought. He watched her reach for the bottle of shampoo and squirt some in her hand. She rubbed her hands together until she had a soft lather and then after smoothing it in his hair, she began washing his long, silky strands in small circles across his scalp.

"No...I, that feels good. No, that was...we bonded tonight. I need to claim you as a wolf. Claim you...claim your nipple." He leaned his head forward and took the pert nipple into his mouth as she continued to thoroughly wash his hair. Her moan nearly had him move his hands, but her hissed "stay" had him gripping harder. He was very glad for the old fashioned tub. Anything less than the cast iron and he would have put permanent finger indentations in it.

"You mean have sex...oh Bradley...what was, oh have sex as wolves? Please. Bradley, I can't think when you do that." Her hands had stilled in his hair as he bit her none too gently. He lathed the area with his tongue and shuddered when she moaned again.

"I can't think when I do this. I need to claim you in the pack meeting place, the stone in the big field." He moved to her other breast. He couldn't seem to get enough of her taste.

"Pack meeting place? Outside? Hummm, I think I might like that, maybe, Bradley, harder! It sounds kind of kinky. Does it feel different as a wolf? Bradley, I want you inside of me." He watched as she rose up on her knees and moved hard against him. His cock was hard and he was aching to be inside her too. When she brushed over his sensitive head with her heated core, he jerked hard upward.

"Not this time. It's required to...please, baby, come down on me, ride me please. I need to be deep inside of you." He was breathing hard, panting, and if his grip got any tighter on the tub's rim, he was going to some serious damage to his fingers.

"Required? Who will be there, Bradley?" She stopped moving again and he couldn't bear it. He unclenched his hands from the sides and wrapped his hands around her waist, lifted her, and settled her down onto him. He moaned as he pulled her onto him.

"Pack. Ride me, Alastriona. Ride me hard." He wanted to be gentle, but she was driving him wild.

"How many pack, all of them?" Cupping her breasts again, he pulled one into his mouth and suckled. The noise he was making against her skin was erotic-sounding to him.

"Half. Can't we talk about this later? You taste much too good to talk about the ceremony right now." His head snapped back. "Ouch! What the hell?" He wasn't sure which hurt more, her handful of his hair or his neck that she had jerked backwards hard.

"How many is half? And I swear to you if you put your mouth on my body once more when I am trying to talk to you, I will castrate you. How. Many. Is. Half?" He felt her hand tighten her hold on his tender scalp.

"They think of you as their queen, you see. And they want to meet you afterwards. David's been getting all kinds of calls. Shit! That hurts!" She had slammed his head back against the tub this time. "Okay, half is about seven, I guess."

"Seven people. I guess that isn't so bad. I mean, I don't want to do that, but...what is it?"

He thought about not correcting her, but he couldn't do it, not now. She'd kill him in front of the entire pack if she showed up and found that he had lied. "Hummm, that's seven thousand, not seven." His head hit the tub hard enough this time that he saw stars. *Mother fuck!*

Chapter Thirty-Three

She tore into the bedroom, water splashing everywhere in her wake. Opening the closet doors and grabbing the first thing she could lay her hands on, she ripped it off the hanger and it went end over end on the rod it was stuck on. "Don't even have my own fucking clothes. Probably expects me to run around bare-assed naked all the time." She was muttering out loud as she pushed buttons through holes. Opening the top drawer of the huge dresser, she pulled out the first thing she laid her hands on and pulled the boxers up over her wet body. She was sort of dressed and out the door before Bradley got out of the tub.

"Ah, Airic, going somewhere?" The vampire Aaron, just great. She was just going to ignore him and keep going, but he proved faster than she was even with a full head of steam driving her.

"Move out of my way or so help me I'll rip your dick off and put it where the sun doesn't shine." She tried to dodge to around him, but he was tricky and fast.

"Not much sun shines on me, love. Bradley, are we trying to make a fashion statement?" She turned to look at him and burst out laughing. He was naked. And when he looked down at himself, she thought he didn't even realize it. She watched in amusement as his face brightened in embarrassment at being caught off guard.

"Do not let her out of this house. So help me, Alastriona, I will paddle you good if you leave before we're finished talking about this." And he turned to run back up the stairs. Presumably, to get dressed, she thought.

Airic turned back to Aaron. She smiled. He looked worried. She smiled bigger and he backed up a step.

"Whatever you're planning, it won't work. I've seen it all, young lady, and there isn't anything…"

***

"Why do they always go for the most sensitive part of the male body is what I'd like to know?" Aaron was being helped up to the couch by Bradley who had just asked the room in general. They had just gotten word from Dom that Airic was with him at Sally the cook's house.

"Because it's the only part that you all seem to think with. Tell me again how she outmaneuvered you." Sara handed him a frozen bag of peas for his groin.

"She's a ninja. I swear I've never seen anyone move like that. One second she was smiling this smile that would make angels weep, the next she had my balls twisted in a sailors knot and was moving me around on my tip toes. And the language! Good heavens, that same sailor who taught her that move also taught her some interesting usage of the English language." She watched as he gently put the peas over his knotted balls.

She was trying hard not to laugh, but it really was too funny. When she had felt Aaron's pain, she'd come

172

running only to find him twisted up on the floor cupping himself, and Bradley standing over him yelling about the incompetence of one ancient vampire being outsmarted by a mere pup.

"What did you say to your mate that pissed her off? We know you bonded with her, hell, the whole house heard you both. Quite enjoyable, actually, but I digress, What did you do?" She smiled at Aaron. The twins were in school and when they'd heard the couple yelling out their release, that had sparked a need in them. And boy, what a spark that had been.

"I tried to explain about the claiming ceremony, but she kept…distracting me. It wasn't right that she expected me to have any kind of grace and have her lick…she was distracting me." He had the good sense to look embarrassed, she thought with a smile. She was a feisty one, his artist.

"That would explain the seven thousand she kept muttering under her breath." Sara turned to the door when Bradley stood, looking at the man in the open way.

"They've lost his scent, Alpha. He's on the loose again. The mistress says she can help."

The first thing Sara noticed was that Airic was pale as death; the second was that she only had eyes for her mate. *Good,* she thought, *very good.*

***

"I don't like this one bit. Why can't she just tell you where the things are and you just pop yourself in and get them then out again?" Bradley had been saying that for the past twenty minutes. Sara was ready to hit him with another tray.

"She's told us and you ten times. She knows exactly where they are and it won't take as long if she goes with him. He won't let anything happen to her, Bradley." She looked over at her mate, who was instructing Airic on how to lead him to the correct room in the house.

She had told them she had painted the man and she had something with his human and wolf scent on it. Aaron had suggested he take her rather than they drive. It was an excellent plan; he would materialize them in the room, get what they needed, and get back out again.

As they watched, they both disappeared. In five minutes, they were back. Airic handed the large canvas to Bradley without a word and the shirt covered in blood to Dom and walked up the stairs to the bedroom. When Bradley made to follow, Aaron stopped him with a shake of his head.

"Wait here. I'll be back." He dematerialized again, but was only gone for a minute or two. When he returned, he had not one, but five more canvases in his hands. He asked them to follow him and went to his study. Sara had never seen him look so serious.

Chapter Thirty-Four

Christopher was pissed. It was all her fault. That damned girl. She was going to be very sorry when he caught up with her. He made her, the ungrateful bitch. She was to whelp his pups, his sons. And what was she doing anyway? Where was she?

"Alpha, you asked to see me?" Christopher looked at Peter. His brother, not only in form, but by blood. He would like nothing more than to shift and tear something, someone apart, but he'd take his fun out on him instead. He smiled.

"That woman, the friend, where is she? I told Simon to bring her to me and he claims she is gone. I want you to bring her to me now. Someone must suffer and since I can't find my errant mate, she will have to do." He sat back in his chair. He hated the chair almost as much as the man who had given it to him, but one did not throw out a gift from one's own sire. It just wasn't done.

"Diana Lake, Alpha. Her name was Diana Lake. She's dead. I'm afraid the wolves who took her were a bit too rough with her and they broke her neck."

He looked down at Peter. Dead. This was her fault too. Her list of punishments was growing by leaps and bounds. "Where is she? I want to destroy her body beyond any recognition. Bring the bitch to me." He leapt up so quickly that he knocked the chair back against the wall and two pictures fell over, crashing to the floor. Peter jumped, but not quick enough to catch the framed photos.

"I'm sorry, Alpha, but she had been discovered already. That Printer person found her and returned her body this morning. It was on the news, another animal attack it was reported to be." He watched as Peter meticulously set the pictures on the credenza.

Fury ripped through him. Christopher growled deep and swept the pictures, all ten of them, to the floor and crashing into the next wall. He shifted then and tore at the room, tearing the sofa seats apart, clawing the walls to the two-by-fours beneath. The carpet was ripped up in places and marked with his scent in others. The chair he hated so much was the only thing not touched. When his anger was spent, he shifted back and surveyed the damage. *Oh she was going to pay all right,* he thought, *and this was just the beginning.*

***

"These were hidden away with the one of the man. I didn't get a chance to see them very well, but I could in her mind. Her pain nearly buckled me when I touched her. I could see what each canvas was depicting there and the horror she felt when she actually saw this happen."

Aaron had set each picture up against the bookshelf in his study in the order she had placed them in her attic. Bradley looked at the church. He'd seen a few pictures of this one in a history book when he was a pup. The cemetery too. He ran his finger gently along one of the headstones and could almost feel the passion she had when she painted it.

The next three took his breath away. The detail was amazing. The terror on Diana's face was horrific; a person could swear he or she could hear her screams coming from her mouth as she was being dragged away by two large wolves. The ones of her family tore him apart. Aaron had said that the paper told they had been attacked by animals, wild ones. But these were weres, there was no doubt about it. They were standing upright while they inflected their carnage. She witnessed this, all of this. He leaned closer to look at the one of her father and knew that the man had been alive as they disemboweled him. He could see the pain plainly written there.

"He was alive. Her father, he was alive when they tore into him. She saw that. She witnessed all of this before she was taken." He stared at them for a few minutes longer and looked at Sara. "Where is she?"

"Bedroom, the one you were in with her. But, Bradley…"

He didn't wait for the rest of what she had to say, but went up to her, taking the stairs three at a time. He knocked on the door this time before opening it. He glanced at Mac, Aaron and Sara's son, who was sitting in the chair by the bed. He knocked on the bathroom door and opened it as well. She wasn't in either of the rooms. He looked again at Mac.

"Where did she go, Mac? Have you seen her?"

He nodded and thrust a sheet of paper at him. Bradley sat down on the floor. He knew before he even opened the primer paper that she was gone.

Bradley,

I have to find Diana; he has her and wants me in exchange. I can't let him hurt another person because of me.

I love you. I know you are mad at me, but I can't sit by and watch another person be destroyed by him.

Alastriona

"Uncle Bradley, Daddy said to come downstairs. He says there is someone here he thinks you should talk to." Mac had left him at some point, he realized, and came back to get him. He wiped at the tears running down his cheeks and rose.

"Tell him I'll be there shortly. I need a few minutes." He walked to the bathroom and started crying in earnest when he realized that the tub they had been playing in was still full of water, and their clothes were thrown about the room. He picked up his shirt she had been wearing and raised it to his nose. *Mine.* And cried harder, soaking the shirt with his tears.

She hadn't trusted him enough to get his help. No, that wasn't it, he realized. She didn't ask because she knew that he'd go after the man and she was afraid he'd be hurt or killed. *Well, that's just too damned bad,* he thought, and stood up. He was her mate, his pack's queen. She'd fucking well better not get herself hurt or he'd paddle her butt but good. With determination and confidence he hadn't felt in years, he left the bedroom, but not before taking off the shirt he had on and putting on the one she had scented.

When he walked into the living room, there stood Peter Alistair, brother to the man who had terrorized his mate. Without thought to the reasons for him being there,

Bradley walked up, grabbed the man by the throat, and lifted him ten inches off the floor. "Where the fuck is your brother and what has he done with my mate?"

Chapter Thirty-Five

"I'm afraid I'm going have to ask you to put him down now. I'd really hate to have to shoot you when you owe us so much money."

He turned slowly without releasing the man. Diana Lake was standing there with a gun pointed directly at his heart.

"She thinks you've been kidnapped by this man's brother and is now going to exchange herself for you. Tell me again why I should let him, or you for that matter, live beyond the next thirty seconds." He shook the man in his grasp before dropping him to the floor. It suddenly hit Bradley. He jerked back around to Peter.

"You're an alpha. That's why you didn't move when I commanded my people to move to Alastriona yesterday." He advanced on the man and watched with disgust as he scrambled away from him.

Aaron loomed before him. "Back off, wolf, or I'll step in." Aaron's eyes had changed and his fangs had dropped and lengthened in his strength and power to control him and not allow him to hurt the other wolf. He wasn't sure he would, but he also didn't know if he could stop himself once he started.

Bradley felt the power now, shimmering in the room. "She is my life! I need her." He fell into the arms of the man in front of him. This was the second time he had taken comfort from this man and he couldn't think of a better friend to have.

"We know where he is. Peter…this is the second time that Peter has saved my life. He can be trusted." Diana sat down on the chair and sobbed.

"I don't understand why you think I'm the alpha. I was born second; Christopher is the older of the two of us." Peter was holding Diana in his arms, comforting her.

"I'm a very powerful alpha; my lineage is very long and strong. The male alphas in the Wolff family have been the leader of the same pack for nearly two thousand years. My command can control a strong alpha and their bitches. You didn't even flinch when I spoke the other day. You should have noticed, but you didn't. You have the ability to control your brother. You are not a second born." Bradley wasn't being arrogant, but rather truthful.

"Why? Why would he lie to me all these years?"

Bradley looked at the man and grinned. Some people were so stupid and prejudice about the dumbest things. "Your eyes are blue. A purebred has brown eyes. He probably took one look at your eye color and made the decision based on that. Tell me, is your mother still alive?" Bradley had an idea that she was not.

"No, why? She died giving birth to me, I was told. That's why my father has always hated me. What does that have to do with anything?" Peter stood now, a little straighter, he noticed.

"I would image that your father thought that she had cheated on him and killed her. He killed her after your brother was born, not you." Bradley didn't care about this man's problems with his family; he wanted his mate back. He had a great deal of groveling to do.

The alpha Peter stood before Bradley and dropped to his knees. In a sign of total submission and faith, he rubbed his neck along Bradley's leg and then rolled to his back, exposing the most vulnerable part of the wolf, both neck and under belly. Peter had just paid the highest compliment that one wolf could give to another.

"I need my mate, Peter. Will you please help me get her back?" Bradley helped the man to his feet and embraced him tight to his chest.

"Yes. He is staying at the Blood Moon in the Merchant district. Do you know where that is?"

Bradley looked to Aaron and threw back his head and laughed. "Oh yes, I know the hotel very well. Very well indeed. I'm part owner in the thing, along with Aaron and two other vampire friends of mine.

"You're a vampire!" With a tiny squeal, Diana dropped to the floor in a dead faint. Peter simply leaned over and picked her up. When he carried her off, following a very flustered Duncan, Bradley turned to Aaron and Sara.

"I think it's high time we call in the troops," he said with a grin.

"Bradley, my dear pup, I do believe you are right. All the troops. How many can you gather of yours in this short of time?" Aaron sat down and pulled out his lists. He had twenty-five vampires that would call the next group of twenty-five who would call the next until he was well fortified.

"It just so happens that I have seven thousand wolves here to see their queen be claimed by their alpha. I don't think they're going to be too happy to hear that she's been kidnapped, not happy at all." Bradley pulled out his cell phone. He would make three calls and within the next hour, they would all be notified. His system was a bit more primal, the Howling a system of a wolf howling to the next with the word would be much faster.

Chapter Thirty-Six

She woke to the sound of screaming, loud and torturous screaming. It was several minutes before she realized it was her. He had her again. Christopher Alistair had grabbed her not ten feet beyond the gate at the MacManus mansion.

Well, he hadn't. A wolf who said that he had been sent by Bradley to follow her had. He had hit her when she fought him and knocked her unconscious. When she woke the first time in this cave, Christopher had thrown his bloodied dead body at her feet.

"This is your fault too, Airic. He shouldn't have hit you, but had you run, I wouldn't have had to send him to bring you home. Then poor...I don't know his name, but it's unimportant. What is is that you are responsible for so much; it may take me years to make you pay." He was pacing as he talked.

She hadn't been hurt by him yet, but it didn't take him long to start. She had quickly learned the hard and painful way not to question him or his judgment.

"How on earth do you figure this is my fault, you moronic ass?" Pow! He punched her in the face. And the beatings began.

She knew his name now. He had told her over and over, having her repeat it every time he hit her; Alpha Christopher Alistair, my mate. She had refused the "my mate" part for as long as she could, but in the end, had said it. He had gone on for an hour on what a great catch he would have been for her, how he had had plans. Plans, he said, that did not include her running away. When she had tried to explain that she hadn't run away but had been rescued, he slapped her across the face again. She was pretty sure he had broken her jaw that time.

She was hanging from a silver chain from the ceiling of what she thought to be a large cave. There was a clamp around her waist as well, and her ankles were braced apart by a metallic bar and clamped to it by silver as well. She knew it was silver because it was burning into her skin like acid.

It was damp in here and cold. And there was very little light. The shirt she had donned…how long ago she didn't know, but it was mostly stripped from her body in tatters. The cat o' nine tails he had used had ripped it to shreds when he had beaten her with it earlier. She could barely stand on her feet and he had beaten the bottoms of them with his belt just after he'd found her. He told her he was going to take what was rightfully his, but he was going to have a bit of fun first.

Moving her head in very slow movements, she saw him in the corner. He was sitting in that damnable chair again. If she, no, when she got out of this, she was going to have the fucker burned. Preferably with him tied to it.

She didn't make a sound, she thought, but must have because he came bounding out of the chair immediately.

"Ah there you are, love. You fell asleep on me earlier and we didn't get the chance to finish our discussion." Fell asleep! She had lost consciousness; the pain had been unbearable. He looked as if he were waiting on a response, so she gave him a weak moan. It was the best she could manage.

He began pacing again, and she closed her eyes. It made her dizzy trying to keep up with his blurry movement. She didn't think he was moving all that fast, it was just a general dizziness.

"As I was saying, you will be punished for every day you were gone. You were a bad girl letting them take you from me. That comes to a total of nearly five hundred and eighty days of punishment for you to receive. And thinking to have sex with that upstart to thrall me was unforgivable of you. I shall have to think long and hard what you shall have to endure for that. You positively reek of him; I doubt I'll ever be able to beat that smell out of you before the end of your life."

She looked up at him then, opening her one good eye. "Kill me later?" She had hoped for a quick death, even after a few days, but to have to wait and be tortured like this for almost six hundred days. She would be dead long before that, she thought, and wondered how he would punish her then. A giggle escaped her mouth. She was as mad as him. As soon as the lash hit her back again, she drifted away into the welcoming blackness.

***

Bradley was slowing going insane himself. He could feel her pain, and whenever he tried reaching out to her, he was blocked. He was sure it wasn't Christopher, but one of his underlings blocking him. Peter had said that his brother had tried to work with magic, something their mother had dabbled in, but had not been able to make the simplest spell work.

"Bradley, are you paying attention? I know you're in pain, but you need to focus. We need your wolves ready when the time is right." Dominic had been called in and was in charge of the hotel. He had been working the security in the building since it had been rebuilt only a few months ago.

"They'll be ready." And they would be too. When the Howling had been sent, he expected his people to be upset and maybe a little angry. News that the alpha's new bitch, a queen alpha at that, had been kidnapped got everyone stirred up, fired up.

He didn't have the seven thousand wolves he had told Aaron he had on hand, but more than likely twice that many. All the neighboring territories had called to give support.

It made him a little nervous. He wondered, not for the first time, what would happen if they didn't find her, or if they didn't find her alive.

"David went by her house today to gather things of hers that would have her scent on it, and there was a...an issue. There were several wolves guarding the house, waiting for her to come home again, he figured. They didn't play well with mine. They're gone; we won't be bothered by them again. But what bothered David was is that they didn't pull away when Christopher took Alastriona. They didn't know. Could he not have her?"

Bradley and his brother had talked about it for an hour this morning before the vampires rose.

"He has her. He just let me know that his bitch is paying her price, but he didn't tell me how or where he has her. I'd like you to teach me how to command him." Peter had walked in the room as Bradley had asked Aaron and Dominic.

Chapter Thirty-Seven

Airic woke up to the sound of music. Classical music. Bach, she guessed. She moved slowly, felt the wounds opening up all over her body, and a tiny moan escaped her throat. She waited for him to say something to her, hurt her in some way. There was nothing. *There mustn't be anyone here,* she thought, for surely she hadn't worked through her punishment schedule yet.

She looked up her arms to her hands and saw that the silver was cutting deeply into her skin. She wondered if she worked hard enough, could she maybe open the vein in her wrist and bleed to death before he came back? But she knew that she wouldn't do it. Well, at least, not yet. Crying softly, she realized she was a coward. She couldn't even end her own life.

"Oh now, we can't have my mate crying now, can we, love? What's the matter, did you miss me? Well, I'm here now. I just thought I'd give you a little more time napping. Thought it'd make our conversation so much longer this time." She heard the whip slither across the rock floor of the cave.

"Please, please don't hurt me anymore. I can't take it. I hurt so badly, please no more." *Begging, I've been reduced to begging,* she sobbed to herself.

She watched as he moved around to her side. He was running the long strips of leather through his fingers as he walked. He was taunting her; he liked her begging. Had she'd been able to, she would have straightened her spine. Fuck this shit. I either die with dignity, or I die a coward.

"You beg so prettily, sweetheart. Of course, it will do you no good. You've made me do this. You've brought this all on yourself. I'm only doing what…"

"Fuck you, you slimy piece of shit. I'm not saying another word to you. I will not beg, I will not moan, you will not get any pleasure from what you, you inflict onto me." She saw it coming, welcomed it as a matter of fact. The fist connected with her mouth so hard it snapped her neck back and opened her lower lip wide. Blood poured from the open wound fresh and hot and poured onto the rock and along a thin seam inside it straight to the earth below.

***

Dominic and Bradley had been going over the maps of the area for nearly six hours. Both were tired beyond anything they could remember for years, but they hadn't stopped. He knew that Dominic would need to rest soon, as he had been up for over twenty-four hours.

Dominic, Aaron, and Colin, all vampires, had mated with magical beings, and it had afforded them special powers that were unique to each of them. Kyle, Tucker, and Tristan, three other vampire friends, had also mated with extraordinary and magical women as well. The one thing that they all received through their mating was the ability to withstand the sun. Not the hottest part of the day, between two and five, but the rest of the day was theirs.

"This is base. I need you to go to section seven dash six and search there. There are three other teams along either side of you." Bradley listened as Scott, one of his pack bodyguards, gave a new location to search for Alastriona.

They had divided up into teams of twenty; ten were to be the main human contacts with radios and the other ten wolves were to search. They had covered a great deal of area and had a lot more to go. Everyone had been working around the clock. He watched as Duncan, the MacManus' butler friend, came in with another tray of sandwiches and drinks.

"My lord, if you don't mind my saying so, you look as though you could use a nap." He took the food offered and set it on his thigh. He had tried to tell him he wasn't hungry earlier, but Duncan had said the new bride would need him to be strong for her when she returned, that he needed to eat. And he did, not realizing until he'd taken the first bite that he actually was very hungry.

"Duncan, my man, I feel like I could use one too." He leaned back in the chair again, thought of nothing but Alastriona while staring at nothing at all. The room moved around him, almost through him, but he didn't take any of it in. It wasn't until a large, tattooed face appeared in front of him not two inches from him that he realized he was being spoken to.

"Welcome back. Feel better?" Colin. Colin was grinning at him. He watched as the man stood—Christ, he was tall—and walked over to the huge map that had been hung on the front of one of the massive bookshelves in Aaron's study.

Bradley sat up and looked around. He must have dozed off for a bit. He actually did feel a little better. He stood and stretched. His wolf moved along with him and he felt the first brush of need. The full moon, it was tomorrow night, well, tonight, he thought.

He went to the patio door and opened it wide. With his excellent night vision, he could see some of his pack members moving along the property. They were guarding their alpha; he could sense that from them. Each member of his household had pledged to find his mate, their queen, this morning. And he believed that they would.

"Bradley! They've found her, sort of. Pete and Shade are on their way here now to show us on the map where they felt her essences enter the earth."

Chapter Thirty-Eight

"Her essences? I don't understand." Bradley knew he had asked that question at least ten times now, but he was anxious and wanted the women to hurry the fuck up. It was either keep repeating himself, or start howling. He figured this was much better for all concerned.

"I don't know, Pete said that they had found her essences and that with the maps, they could finally direct us in the correct direction. Sit down, Bradley, before I have to hurt you. You've been pacing for the past fifteen minutes and it won't make them get here any faster."

He wanted to snarl at Aaron, but he knew he was right. He sat down. Then he popped right back up again and went to the door. He knew it wasn't them, his wolves would have warned him when a car pulled into the drive, but damn it...

"They are at the gate. If you behave yourself and not rush them, I'll let you go to the door," Aaron said to him while he was gripping tightly to his shoulders.

"I'm not a child, stop treating me like one." But he could feel his heart pounding in his chest in a hard, painful thump.

"Bradley, your canines have been down since Colin told us the women found something. Your hair looks like you've been running your…paws through it for days, not just hours. Get a grip, you're kinda scaring my kids. And you stink. Badly."

He looked over to where Aaron and Sara's six-year-old twins were huddled on the couch. They were looking at him like he was going to shift at any moment and eat them alive. He didn't like that look. He pulled his wolf closer to him and soothed him. He felt him curl around the warmth of his body like a caress. Taking a deep, cleansing breath he looked back at him. "I…I'm sorry Aaron. I need her."

"Yes, and she'll need you. The women will need to look over the maps with Scott and Dominic. Go take a shower and put on some fresh clothes. I'm begging you. Actually, we're all begging you, to take a shower. You smell like a wet dog."

Smiling stupidly, he took off for the stairs and went up them two at a time. He couldn't remember the last time he'd showered and shaved. And that was bad. He would shower, but shaving would have to wait.

Bradley went to the bedroom he and Airic had shared so much. He would get her back. Turning on the hot water, he stripped down to his bare skin. He glanced at his mark, the mark that had made him the true alpha.

When the oldest male was born in the Wolff family, he was born with a mark. It was a small wolf foot print about an inch wide and two inches high, just over his heart. When the male pup went through puberty, the mark changed to a deep red and grew another inch each way. Sometimes, like in this generation of Wolffs, the second male child would be born with the same mark. Most times, it didn't grow, but faded over time, and by the time they reached adulthood, the mark would be completely gone.

David had been born with the same mark as Bradley. When David had reached puberty, like his older brother, his grew as well, but had not changed to the deep red as his brother's had. David's had turned a royal blue, marking him as a protector, a wolf pack enforcer.

Bradley leaned in closer to the mirror and studied his mark now. It was different. He looked at his tribal, the one the eldest of the pack had tattooed into his arm when he had taken over the pack and become the alpha. It too had changed. He needed to talk to his grandda, and started to leave the bathroom, but realized that he hadn't showered yet. He stepped under the spray. He washed his hair and then his body. He leaned his back against the shower stall wall and stood there for a minute. Then he moved under the hot spray for five minutes more, sobbing hard, his heart hurting.

He hurried down the stairs to find the one man he knew would have the answers he needed. Bradley needed the man who meant more to him than any other man on the planet, his grandda, his best buddy.

"Grandda, I need to show you something." He had dried quickly and dressed in the first thing he found in the drawers.

He had brought clothes over here some time ago because he would shift to wolf before leaving the pack house and run here sometimes late at night. Rather than sit around talking to Aaron in the raw, he'd slowly brought a few sets of clothes over to change into. He had pulled on a pair of sweatpants and a ratty t-shirt with a band on it that he'd heard in maybe college.

His grandda followed him into the large entrance hall. He pulled the shirt over his head and showed him the marks.

His grandda staggered back a few steps and Bradley leaped forward to grab him. He helped him sit down in the large church pew near the door and started fanning him. He had gone so pale that he feared for his life.

"Grandda, let me get Grams. I won't be but a second, all right? Don't move." Bradley started to rise, but the hand on his shoulder stayed him. Looking behind him at the owner. He was surprised to see Mel.

"Ah, so the king is born. Welcome King of all Wolves, Alpha Bradley. I have been waiting for you." Mel bowed before him.

Chapter Thirty-Nine

The water splashed over her face and arms, waking her. The jerk from the cold water made her nearly moan, but she had remembered her promise to him. She said nothing, made no sound at all.

This was the third, or maybe the fourth time he had woken her this way. The only thing he had succeeded in doing was washing her blood off her. He had given up threatening her and had just been beating her senseless until she passed out again. She knew that he stopped when she was out because he had told her once before that he wasn't going to waste his time hurting her if she couldn't feel it.

She did, though. All of it. She was sure that he had broken nearly every rib and her arms and legs. The fact that she could heal quickly was to his advantage in that he could break them again once they healed. But she was getting weaker and weaker, and it was taking her longer and longer to heal each time. Airic was dying, very slowly, she was dying.

"You'll scream this time, scream and scream. I've got a special punishment for you now, my love."

She watched dispassionately as he walked over to a small fire he had started. She hurt so badly in so many places that even if he set her afire, she wouldn't know if she'd feel it. He came toward her with a white-hot rod, and even before he told her, she knew he meant to burn her with it.

***

"We've found her. We know where she is."

Bradley looked at Peter and stared at him blankly for several seconds. They found her; they found her, three of the sweetest words he'd ever heard.

"You cannot go, Alpha; you must stay behind and come to her after they find her. It's important that you heed me in this."

Mel had to be crazy if she thought he'd wait to go to her. He turned to her to tell her what she could do with her heeding advice.

"Bradley, listen to her. There are things you must do to lead. One of the things you must do to be a great leader is listen. Trust me, son."

His grandda too? Were they all nuts? Leave her to someone else. "She's my mate. Their queen, and you want me to stay behind. I don't fucking think so. I'm going to go to her. And I'm going to bring her home. I'd like to see you try and stop me." He watched as Peter backed out of the hall and returned to the study.

Mel watched too as Peter left the room, he noticed. Then when she turned back to him, she looked sad. He knew he wasn't going to like what she said to him. Knew it as surely as he was standing there.

"Peter is a good man, don't you think? I do. He isn't a great man, not like you, but a good man." She sat down beside his grandda.

"Yeah, I suppose. But just so you know, I'm not buying the flattery. So keep it out of this." He started pacing. It was better than hitting the wall with his fist.

"It isn't flattery, it's the truth. He could be a great man, if you'd let him. The Fates have said that he will be a great help to you in the years to come if he becomes the man that his father killed. You have given him the tools to become that man. Now he needs the knowledge that he can and will be him. Are you willing to sacrifice this one thing to him? It is up to you, alpha king. You can decide to go and I will do nothing to stop you. But sometimes, a great leader doesn't lead, but allows others to lead for him." He watched as she touched his grandda and saw the change in him immediately. She had healed whatever had made him ill.

He walked to the study without answering her. The Fates. The Fates had given him Alastriona, he had no doubt about that. She had needed the comfort of a laugh, and they had given her the blue house. He needed to give someone else the blue house.

"Dom, I need you to go with Peter, can you do that for me?" Bradley hated this with every fiber of his being. She needed a laugh and he needed her, and that thought alone would get him through this.

"Anything you say, Alpha."

He took a deep breath. He watched as Peter worked with Dom on how to get to the cave. "Peter, I want you to go with Dom." He looked at his grandda and then a Mel.

She nodded once at him. "I need you to bring my mate back to me and handle your brother."

Chapter Forty

Peter and Dom left the MacManus mansion about forty minutes later. They were to gather as many wolves as they needed on the way. Bradley had already sent a message to every one of his wolves telling them that they had found their queen and that they were to support Peter, as they would him. No one had objected or balked. He hadn't really thought they would, but things were tense and he needed them.

He was to follow in the car behind them with Thomas Reilly, MD, a vampire, and the new doctor they had hired, Leif Bergeron, who was human, at the clinic they had just built. She would need medical attention and they were taking no chances with her health.

Bradley could keep in touch with his own wolves, but the others, the ones from other realms, he wasn't so sure. Dom would make sure that he was kept apprised of the situation and let him know if they needed anything.

He didn't know if he was going to be able to sit still for very long, but at the last minute, Aaron had decided to come with him. The two doctors sat in the back and Aaron in the front with him.

"Have you thought about what you are going to do with Christopher when he's caught?" Christopher had committed his crimes in his territory. It would be up to Bradley to decide how best to deal with the situation. He glanced over at him.

"You mean if there's anything left of him when the others find him? No. I mean, I'd like to tear him apart with my bare hands, but I'm not so sure that would be justice or revenge. What would you do?"

"Tear him apart. No question." Bradley grinned at him.

***

At first, she thought she was hearing things. It wouldn't be the first time over the past few days, weeks, or years for all she knew. The pain had become her sole focus. But she had never heard the sound of wolves before; at least she was pretty sure she hadn't. It might have frightened her at any other time, but now it was just a different sound.

There was no one inside the cave but her when the first large wolf moved into the room. She realized after a few seconds of him staring at her that she could hear him, his thoughts.

"Are you alone, my lady? Is Christopher here?"

Her mind wanted to rebel at this, because she knew that he wasn't asking her in a real verbal language, but as wolf. Like the guard in the hospital so many months ago, she also knew that she would be able to speak back to him.

"No, I don't think so. Please, you have to leave. He'll kill you if he finds you here. I can't save you if he returns."

"I've come to take you to your alpha; Bradley has sent me for you." Peter moved behind her and shifted. Airic felt the stir in the air, magic, she supposed. He moved in front of her, dressed in a pair of workout shorts and flip-flops. "Oh, mistress, I'm so sorry. Bradley is coming, and he's bringing help for you. I need to get you down from these chains; they've cut deeply into your arms. Dom has some water for you if you'd like."

"Bradley? Dry. Hurt. Badly. No. No touch." Each word felt as if she were ripping it from her throat. She didn't want him to stay, but she didn't want to be left alone again either. *Bradley,* her mind screamed. *He'll come.*

The second and third wolf entered and filled the mouth of the cave with their size. Each one had a bright silver streak down their left flank and huge paws. *Oh, Grandma, what big teeth you have,* she thought.

Airic couldn't lift her head, and her arms were useless. And since they had been over her head for however long she had been here, she knew that they would be painful when she was cut down. Breathing was difficult too. "Leave. Leave me."

Ignoring her, he only worked at the chain. Each movement rang through her body, filling her with such agony that she couldn't think beyond it.

When he touched her arm, she couldn't help it, she screamed and lost consciousness.

Chapter Forty-One

Bradley sat for a full minute before he could move out of the car. She was just inside there; his love was just feet away. Opening the door, he slipped out of the Hummer.

The first thing he noticed was that each wolf he passed bowed before him and wouldn't look at him. He knew those who had seen her were horrified at the way she had been tortured. He had heard from Dom, although alive, she was in a terrible state. He had said that while her heartbeat was slow, it was strong. And once she lost consciousness, they were able to work quicker at getting her loose from the bonds.

Inside the cave, he could smell the stench of blood, sweat, and urine. There was a crowd of people just around her, but they moved away as he got closer, except for Thomas. He stood in front of him before he could see her.

"Bradley, look at me. She's not just been beaten, she's been tortured too. What he's done to her...Bradley, it's very bad. She needs medical attention more than I can give her here. If we try to move her, I fear she will die. She can't shift; she isn't strong enough to survive it. She needs blood, strong vampire blood to survive."

Bradley gently moved him aside and knelt down beside her. "Alastriona, love, can you hear me?" He moved his finger down her cheek and she cringed slightly away from him. He felt tears stream down his face.

She was broken, her face was bloody and raw, and burn marks from something being laid against her skin were along her tender cheek and throat. Her nose, jaw, and cheekbone had been shattered; one eye was swollen shut the other barely open, just a slit. There was blood coming from her ear, and also blood in her hair, red from it. She was covered by a blanket so he couldn't see the extent of the damage done to her there, but her blood soaking through nearly everywhere showed that she had suffered the same injuries done to her face all over her body.

"Bradley, Bradley, we need to talk. We can't stay here. What do you want us to do?" Aaron had knelt beside him and put a hand on his shoulder. He wanted to cradle her into his arms and hold her, but he knew that he would likely kill her if he did.

"Aaron, could you heal her? Your blood is strong and Thomas said that's what she needs to survive. I have to…she has to survive, Aaron. I cannot live without her." Unashamed of the tears, he allowed them to go unchecked, unmindful of the others who saw.

"My blood…it isn't the same anymore. I…yes, I can help her, but I need a favor, a boon in exchange. That's what the magic needs to make it work. Bradley, there could be changes in the two of you if you do this because you will need to sip from me or Sara as well. And this exchange will allow me to find her and you, contact you as I do my vamps, you understand?"

Bradley looked back down at the woman on his lap. He needed her, but more than that, he was deeply in love with her. "Whatever it takes. Yes, whatever you want. I give you my word, whatever you want, it's yours. Please, please, I beg you to save my mate. I cannot, no, I won't live without her." He touched her again, softer this time.

"Sara is coming. She will feed you, and I, your mate. She will need to give her own boon when I ask."

Bradley watched as Aaron opened the vein at his wrist and put it to her mouth. His blood flowed quickly into her mouth, but she wasn't swallowing. It dripped out the corner of her lips. For long, tense minutes, no one moved or spoke. They all knew, knew that if she didn't drink, they couldn't move her. If they couldn't move her, then there was no medical help for her. She would die.

He moved his fingers to her throat and began to rub it up and down. He tried his best to ignore the way his fingers slid along the long column and the fact that it slid easily because of the blood, her blood. He felt the first swallow, then the next. It wasn't until she drank a full half dozen mouthfuls that he breathed. He looked up at his friend and when Aaron winked at him, he nearly burst into tears again.

"She'll live now. She'll heal soon. In an hour, you should be able to move her to shelter and safety. I need to go back to the mansion, but I will come at sunset. Sara will be here soon." Bradley felt the stir of magic and glanced over at the absence of his friend. Aaron had dematerialized to his home.

Chapter Forty-Two

Airic opened her eyes. This wasn't a room she was familiar with, neither was the bed. She gingerly slid her legs along the sheets. The pain was there, but not entirely unbearable. Moving her arms, the pain was a little more, but again, nothing like she was used to over the past several days. She turned her head and saw an elderly gentleman sitting in a large, overstuffed chair beside the bed, and he was napping. The short whiskey glass he had in his hand was very close to tipping its amber contents onto his lap. There was a lit cigar in the ashtray on the stand next to him. The ash was fairly long, so she assumed he'd been napping for some time. She must have made a noise because he came awake suddenly and looked right at her.

"Well, hello there. How you feeling? Aaron said you'd be better quickly. Didn't believe it, but there you are."

She moved a little straighter in the big bed and winced. He hopped up so quickly she jerked back and moaned this time. She tried to relax because when she tensed, the muscles protested and it hurt. He reached out and put his hands to her waist when she whimpered at him. She knew deep down that he wasn't going to hurt her, but she had hurt been hurt so badly. She started crying a little when he sat down on the bed.

"Here now, now that won't do. Bradley won't like this. There now, honey, you're safe now. You'll be fine." He was patting her hand and speaking softly to her.

"Bradley. Where?" The little bit she had moved had worn her out. She laid back on the pillows and felt the tears fall down her cheeks.

"He's gone to get something to eat down in the kitchen. He hasn't been gone long, but he'll be back soon. I'm Charlie Wolff, his grandda. You've only been here since about nine this morning; it's now…four-thirty. You need anything?" She watched him rise, then go over to the chair he had been sitting in.

"I hurt. Everywhere." She moved again, and realized that she didn't hurt as badly has she had before. "Not as bad now." Her throat really hurt. It was a few seconds before she remembered why. He had put that red hot pike to her neck. She shuddered.

"You should be much better by tomorrow and completely healed in a few days. Grandda, can I have a few minutes with her, please?" She looked to the door as soon she felt him coming up the stairs. *Felt him,* she thought. And she realized that she needed to touch him, have him touch her.

"You leaving me?" She leaned back against the pillow again and watched him move toward her slowly. When he sat down on the bed next to her, she reached out to touch him and felt a hum run through her.

"No, no, I'll never leave you. You look amazing, so beautiful. I love you, baby. I'm so happy you're all right."

He touched her face, ran his fingers down her cheek and along her neck.

"Please. Bradley, kiss me." She leaned forward and touched her mouth to his, gently first then with more possession. She moaned when he pushed her back against the headboard.

"As much as I want to finish this, to make passionate love to you, we can't. I can see that this has exhausted you already. God, I can't believe I'm saying this, but I don't want to have sex right now. Well, that's not really true. I want you fully recovered before we have sex. When we make love, it will with both of us able to enjoy it fully, you understand?"

"Yes. I understand. I love you. The full moon, tonight?" She was tired, she realized. But he loved her. She could do anything.

"Yes. It's tonight and you will stay here and rest. The wolf, our pack, understands what you've been through. They're all so happy that you're fine and home again. The next meeting will be fine with them for us to...you know."

"Have sex in front of seven thousand, is that what you mean?" She closed her eyes for just a second just to rest them and when she opened them again it was full dark outside. A quick look at the clock across the room showed that it was almost nine-thirty. Shit. She moved to the side of the bed and stood up slowly.

"I hope that you plan to wear more than that. You are going to the pack meeting, aren't you? I thought so. I brought you something pretty to wear." She turned to the woman who she would swear had not been there five seconds ago.

"Who are you, and how do you know what I'm going to do?" She had to sit down again. Okay, she wasn't all that strong, dizzy as a matter of fact, she thought.

"I am Melody, Mistress of Light, and Keeper of All Magic and all that jazz. I know everything. Well, most everything. There are the Fates, those wonderful women who make decisions and don't share them with me, but that's another issue altogether. I have this outfit for you to wear. And I know someone who will help you get there." Airic watched her walk across the room and lay the garment bag on the chair. Then she sat on the bed.

"And I should trust you, why?" She scooted over and leaned back against the headboard. Her body was feeling better, but she knew that what Bradley had told her earlier was true; she would take a few days to heal.

"It needs to end tonight, Alastriona Airic Bennett, and you are the power to end it."

Chapter Forty-Three

"My name, someone did that before...that woman, Aaron's wife, she said my whole name like you just did. Then she zapped me. Why, why do I feel they go together? That you two are together?" Airic stood up, walked over to the bag and touched it, then turned to Mel.

"Very good, Airic, very good indeed. There is power in a name. When you know the person's real name, you hold a power over them that others do not. When you need to issue...say, a command and you want to add some kick ass power, just say the name with it."

"And this outfit, what does it have to do with this ceremony?"

"Dom has agreed to take you to Bradley, but you'll need to tell him to. He is very devoted to you, by the way. He will make sure you get there safely. As soon as you are ready, he'll make sure that you go to the correct place." Mel walked to the door, turned, then looked at Airic. "Before you go to him, have Dom take you to Bradley's study." She shut the door quietly behind her.

Airic picked up the bag and hung it on the back of the bathroom door. She turned on the shower, stripped down, and stepped under the spray. The water felt good sliding down her skin. She picked up the shower poof and poured a generous amount of the creamy soap into it. She started to wash her arm when she noticed a medium-sized bruise on her chest, just over her heart. She really couldn't see it very well, and after a mental shrug, she washed her other arm and her torso. When she rubbed the soapy poof over her legs, she remembered the mark around her thigh. She remembered the sensual feeling she received when Bradley had touched it, the feeling that had run through her entire body.

The tattoo went all the way around her thigh and was about two inches wide. The detail and colors were fantastic. It was of gray and black wolves chasing each other, one right after the other. Sometimes they were up on hind legs; others were in mid-run. The ground they ran on changed as it encircled her, going from a scene from spring, fading to summer, into fall, and ending in winter.

When she was drying off, she moved closer to the mirror and noticed that the dark spot wasn't a bruise after all, but another mark. This one was a perfect paw print in a deep, deep blood red, and with an outline of gold that was so thin that unless one was very close to it, no one would see it. It was about two inches wide and three inches tall.

She opened the garment bag and pulled out the dress. It was very beautiful. At the bottom of the bag were a strapless bra and a thong of the same color as the dress, which was the same deep red hue as the mark she'd found on her chest.

The bodice of the dress had buttons down the front and had no straps as it modestly draped over her breasts. It wasn't tight, but it did fit well enough that she didn't need anything to hold it up. When she slipped it on, she noticed that her paw print was openly displayed. The waist was tight and belted with a narrow silver chain. The skirt simply dropped from the waist to the top of her thigh and hinted above the tattoo around her leg. It looked as if the dress had been made especially to show off her new marks, but she knew that wasn't possible as she had just discovered the marks herself. She slipped on the black toeless sandals and moved toward the door as she pulled her hair back away from her face. She didn't bother with braiding it because she knew that Bradley liked it down. When she opened the door, there just across the hall from her stood Dom.

He dropped to the floor before her and rubbed his neck along her bare leg. She felt the warmth of this action run through her, leaving her feeling his respect and awe at her. It was an odd feeling.

"My queen. You look very lovely, if I may say so. Mistress Mel said to take you by Alpha's office. If you're ready, we'll go there now." He waited for her to precede her down the stairs.

"I don't know where we're going, Dom, so you lead. I'm not sure what she wanted me to do or see, do you?" She walked beside him rather than behind. When she looked up at him, she noticed that he had on a deep red sash at his waist, but before she could ask him about it, he was opening the door. She walked inside and before she could find the switches for the lights, he flipped them on and then walked out of the office, closing the door behind him. She walked around for a few minutes before she saw the vase, her vase. Bradley had her original vase, the one with the tress on it.

She walked slowly over to it, not believing that after all this time, she now knew who had purchased the first piece she had ever sold. He was the buyer she couldn't find. She ran her finger down one of the limbs on the tree.

Chapter Forty-Four

Bradley looked around the open field. Despite being told that his mate would not be able to appear, thousands had shown up. This was by far the biggest crowd that had ever attended the full moon. He sat on the ceremonial rock and thought about her.

She had looked so much better when he'd left her a couple of hours ago. So much better that he'd wanted to skip this altogether and just stay with her. But his grandda said that his pack would be very upset by that, so here he was.

"She'll be fine, you know. You left more than two dozen men with her and another dozen roaming the grounds. No one will get to her, no one would dare."

He looked over at his grams. He hugged her to him and kissed her. "I know, but I didn't assign anyone to stay behind but Dom. And I didn't really have to ask him, he told me he was staying. The others decided to stay with her on their own. I'm not sure how many more would have stayed if I hadn't insisted that some of them come and represent the pack."

"They love her. Her courage is something that they are proud of, her strength. They're in awe at how much she suffered as his hand. Have they found him yet?"

Bradley looked out over the crowd. "No, not yet, but we will." He heard the excitement rippling through the crowd. He wasn't sure what was going on, but he stood in front of his grams to protect her. When the crowd parted and he saw Dom carrying Airic, he nearly leapt at her. He wasn't sure whether he wanted to grab her for himself, or shake her for coming out so soon. He settled for growling at Dom.

"Don't you dare be mad at him. I made him bring me here, and you know I can too. He likes me enough not to leave me in the house by myself."

He looked up at the man who was now sitting her down on the rock beside his Grandmother.

"The queen wasn't by herself, Alpha. There were perhaps sixty wolves within twenty feet of her at all times." He bowed away, but only as far as behind the rock she was sitting on.

Bradley looked at her and tried to be mad. But he just couldn't pull it off. Instead, he leaned down and captured her mouth with his. The kiss wasn't near long enough, nor deep enough, but they both felt the heat of it. When she growled in her throat at him, he nearly pushed her back on the rock and took her right there. As it was, he was very glad for the loose-fitting lounge pants that he traditionally wore to these events. His cock had surged to awareness of her as soon as he touched her.

He noticed that there wasn't any noise behind him and turned, still bent over her to look at his people. Turning back to see the expression on Airic's face, he nearly laughed out loud. She looked like she'd been caught with both hands in the cookie jar before dinner.

"Alastriona, what do you want me to tell them? They want their queen, tonight. But if you aren't up for it then they will understand. They'll be disappointed, but they'll understand. The stories surrounding your torture will be something they tell their own children's children."

"They truly will, dear. I've never seen a…Airic, you're marked! I…I've never…Bradley, quickly take off your shirt. I need to see, are you marked as well?" She started tugging at his shirt and when he pulled it over his head, she stood to look at his print.

"Grams, what is it? Mel said I'd been born finally; I never got a chance to ask her what she meant. And who marked Alastriona?" He pulled Airic to her feet and held her close to him as he looked at her marking that was the exact duplicate of his, size, color, and location.

"You are the true king and queen of the wolves. It has been said that you would come and lead your people with a woman worthy of you at your side. She is even dressed in the traditional colors and style befitting the queen. Where did you get this, dear?"

When Airic put her arms around his waist and pulled him closer to her, he responded in kind.

"This queen somebody brought it by and said I was to come here. It needed to be finished tonight. I'm not sure what she meant, but I wanted to be with Bradley, so here I am."

Bradley kissed her head. His queen. He watched as his grandda came forward, Mel at his side. He'd never seen him look so happy in all his life. When he started to stand on the stone, he moved to give him a hand up and moved back to Airic when he waved him away. Grams moved to his side when he held out his hand to her. The crowd, already quiet, silenced at the raising of his hand.

"Today we rescued our alpha's mate. We all brought her home and helped her heal. The man who kidnapped and hurt her is still at large, but we will get him." Grandda waved his hands again to silence the crowd. They had cheered at his declaration. "But tonight...tonight, we are here to celebrate. Our alpha has found his true mate. A woman with great courage and strength. A woman who would sacrifice her own life for others. But that isn't all. I have just been informed that they carry the mark of royalty, that the marks of their race have changed and made them leaders of all time. Our alpha and his bitch have been marked as our king and queen. Tonight, when he claims is mate, our alpha claims your queen, our queen. Tonight, it is my greatest honor and privilege to present to you Bradley and Alastriona Wolff."

Before the crowd could react to the news, there was a single clapping. Bradley turned to look at the source and pushed Airic behind him.

"So lovely of you to bring everyone here for my claiming of my mate. Bitch, you are going to pay for this." And the whip lashed out toward Airic.

Chapter Forty-Five

Before anyone could react, Bradley had the whip in his hand. He had jerked it away from Christopher so quickly that the other man didn't have time to fight him for it.

Terror ran through Airic so deeply that she couldn't breathe or move for several precious seconds. His voice had chilled her, terrified her, and brought back the memories and pain like it was happening all over again.

She watched in abject horror as Dom rushed the wolf and was slashed across this throat and thrown back against a tree several feet away. He had been protecting them, her. She wanted to help, needed to help, but she was too terrified to move. No matter how much she begged her body to move, it wouldn't.

Bradley moved forward to challenge him, she was sure to kill him, when a shot rang out. Bradley dropped to the ground, blood pouring from a wound in his stomach. The smoking gun in Christopher's hand helped her in a way she would never had thought possible.

"Stop! You will not move another step. Drop the gun. Now!" She could hear the command in her voice, and

223

apparently, so could he. She watched as he started to move, to fire the gun again at her beloved. Glancing quickly at the wolves behind him, she spotted Leif, the doctor who had come to see her today.

"See to them. Christopher Felix Alastair, you will drop that weapon now! You have shot the alpha of this pack, what do you have to say for yourself? And do not lie to me." She stepped forward when the gun dropped from his now limp hand and kicked the gun away. She looked over at the doctor and at his nod that Bradley and Dom would be all right, she turned back to the man who had hurt them.

"You bitch! When this night is over, my name will be on the lips of every wolf in the country. Every bitch will know what I am, who I am. I will be remembered for all that I have done. I killed him, just like I'm going to kill you. I am the alpha, the greatest wolf of all time." He looked as if he really believed what nonsense he had just imparted. He probably did, she thought. Well, I can help him with that. Smiling, she raised her hand toward him.

"Shift." She watched as his body twisted and shaped into a wolf. His screams of pain could be heard all the way to the back of the pack. It did not move her. She felt nothing as she watched his bones break and reshape into a wolf. Nothing at all when his jaw lengthened and stretched, teeth filling in where there hadn't been any before. When he finished, a mere three seconds later, he lay there panting and whimpering.

"I have not yet been claimed by your alpha, so it isn't within my rights to kill this wolf. I give to you, pack of the Brotherhood of Gray, his punishment as you see fit. You may render your own judgment against him and carry through on the punishment that fits the crime. I only ask that wolf should deal with wolf." She turned her back to him and the crowd and dropped before Bradley. He was sitting up against the stone and watching her.

She never took her eyes off the man before her when she heard the crowd shift as one, the magic rippling along the air like a lover's caress. She never stopped her forward motion to his mouth as Christopher started barking and snarling at the approaching pack, their own vicious growls soon overriding his. When her mouth covered his, her tongue swept against his, she didn't so much as flinch when the scream he issued was cut off with the sound of breaking bones. It was over in a matter of seconds.

Christopher Felix Alastair was no more.

Chapter Forty-Six

"I claim you, Alastriona Airic Bennett, as my mate before my pack. I claim you, Alastriona Airic Bennett, as the alpha bitch to my pack, the Brotherhood of Gray. I claim you, Alastriona Airic Bennett, as my true love, the woman of my heart. I will protect you with my life. I will honor you with my heart. Alastriona Airic Bennett, with your permission, I claim you as my bride in the way of our people, of our clan. Do you accept me as you mate?"

It was full dark now. The moon was high in the sky and shining full and bright down on the couple standing near the stone, looking only at each other. Bradley's voice carried well to every wolf standing there waiting for them, waiting for her to say yes and become one with their alpha.

"Yes, Bradley Thornton Wolff, I accept. I will give my life for yours and each member of our pack. I will stand beside you throughout eternity. You are my heart, my life, and my love. I love you, Bradley Thornton Wolff."

He winced; he wondered first of all who was kind enough to help her with the verse that would unite them and then who he was going to have to kill because they had given her his middle name. He glanced over at David and knew without a doubt his brother had sold him out. He was so dead after this. He looked at Airic and realized that his grin might have been a little to manic for this right now. "I love you, but I'm killing David tomorrow," he told her as he kissed her.

Now was the hard part for her, he knew. They would need to undress and shift, then as wolves, he would need to claim her. He gently turned her around and with her back to his chest, he began.

Kissing her neck just where her shoulder met her neck, he reached around her and slowly unbuttoned the top to her dress. He wanted her to forget the people, wolves watching them. Maybe if he made this just the two of them, she'd be less nervous.

"Bradley, we'll never make it as wolves if you keep touching me this way. Let me shift and we do this. Then I want to take you back to the house and fuck you all night."

He grinned at the howling of the wolves around them. "They can understand you now, you know? Once you took me into you and agreed to be their bitch, they now understand you as well as they do me." When she stiffened slightly then shrugged, he knew she was going to be fine.

He had stopped unbuttoning her and watched as she turned toward him and finished off the task of removing the dress. His mouth dried up. She stood before him in the skimpiest little bra he'd ever seen, and her panties were nothing more than a triangle between her legs and two strings at her hips.

"Fuck me," he breathed quietly, and stood admiring her luscious body. His cock hardened in his pants, and when he thought of taking her as his wolf, he nearly leaped atop her.

When she reached between her breasts to free them, he stopped her. Enough was enough, and she didn't have to bear anymore of herself to the crowd. Besides, he could feel the lust rising from them, especially from the younger wolves. He would be very surprised if there wasn't a huge increase in his pack ten months from tonight.

"Shift, love. Shift now." He could tell the moment she felt it too. Her body responded to the scents and pheromones in the air. When he felt the first ripple of her shift run along his skin, he pulled his wolf forward too. Their shift was quick and beautiful.

He moved along her body with his larger one and marked her with his coat. This scent wouldn't last long, only until they shifted back, but any wolf coming upon her would know that she was not only claimed, but who had claimed her. No one, wolf or human, would touch her again.

When he moved along her neck, pressing his against hers, she lifted her muzzle in the air and gave him her throat to nip. He needed to draw her blood so that his pack could smell it. It wasn't much, only a few drops, but it was enough to get them into a frenzy of howling.

He moved behind her and could smell her arousal, her need. He had made love to her before, but this was different. She couldn't be a participant in this, but would have to submit to his dominance over her.

"Alastriona Airic Bennett, I love you." He swept through her mind, giving her his need, showing her what he wanted, needed from her.

"Please, Bradley, please now," she purred back into his mind.

His cock hardened and readied for her. He moved up behind her and pressed her shoulders down against the ground as he covered her. She resisted at first and he sank his teeth into her shoulder. Surging forward, he entered her. His cock went deep and he felt her tightness around him. He rocked into her again and felt her responding to him. Not pulling his canines from her, he fucked her hard and quick. It wasn't long before he could feel himself ready for his release into her. She wouldn't be able to come this way, or so he thought, until she started whimpering and moving back against his thrusts. He pumped harder and harder into her until he felt her explode beneath him, pulling him along with her. His cum jettisoned into her, hot, hard, and fast. Over and over he pumped his seed into her womb until he emptied himself and collapsed atop her.

Neither of them moved for long moments and would probably have stayed that way longer if the pack had not brought them back to earth with their howls of approval. They had their queen; Bradley had his mate.

Chapter Forty-Seven

It was several hours and nearly dawn before they made it to the cabin in the woods. David had told them that he had had it prepared for them, stocked it with food and fire wood. He said that some of the women had gone up just today and cleaned it up. He admitted that he hadn't thought about it being closed up for all this time until Donna had said something about the dirt.

Bradley and Airic had run as wolves with the pack for hours after the claiming. He had taken her twice more, in private this time, and in wolf form, both of them nearly cross-eyed with need both times. She wanted him as a man, but was enjoying this time together as wolves.

She had never run with another wolf before, always hiding and keeping to herself when she had to change. And having an entire pack to run with was something she had enjoyed completely. They had run and played, splashed through the shallow waterways, and had even chased a deer or two. Once they had come upon a scent that was familiar, but not welcome, and Bradley had simply lifted his leg and marked the area with his own scent, bringing peals of laughter from her.

When they got to the cabin, they shifted and were suddenly shy with each other. They had had sex as animals, but now as humans, they didn't know what to do, how to be a couple. He suggested they move out to the hot tub and relax. There was an outdoor shower just outside the enclosed tub area that they rinsed off in. The shower water was very cold, so when they sank into the hot water of the hot tub, it was wonderfully welcome to their bodies.

"Thank you for allowing Diana to be there during the ceremony. It was nice having someone there I knew." She was sitting across from him in the huge tub.

"You're very welcome. Peter asked me tonight if he may take her as his mate. I asked if she was and he said yes. I told him that it would be up to her. He said that he is going to convince her over the next few days. He is going to become the alpha of his brother's pack, as he should have been before." He watched her. She was looking at everything but him.

"She'll make a good mate. She already knows more about weres than anyone I know. Well, knew anyway." Again, she stared off into the dawning day.

"What's wrong, Alastriona?" He moved to sit beside her and then pulled her onto his lap with her back against his chest. He wanted her, wanted to make love with her, but she seemed a little upset and he wanted to figure out why.

"Nothing. Well, I..." She turned around and straddled his legs with her thighs, her hands on his shoulders. He rested his hands on her waist and waited for her to continue. Or kiss him.

"Alastriona, we need to be honest with each other. And we have to be able to talk to each other. We have a very large pack to oversee and I need you by my side. My side love, not behind me."

"Am I your mate because Christopher changed me, or am I your mate because I am? Do you love me because I'm Airic, or because I'm your mate? I'm frightened, Bradley, terrified that you'll come to realize that I'm a fraud and leave me." She laid her head on his shoulder and nuzzled him there.

"Alastriona, if you keep doing that, I won't be able to answer you. I love you because you're my mate who also happens to be Airic. You're my mate because he changed you and the Fates decreed it. You aren't a fraud, love. A fraud would never have been able to pull his wolf tonight with only a word. Nor would any other female have been able to command so many to do what they did for you tonight. You are their alpha and they bow to you as they would me." He couldn't help himself, he tried to behave, but he wanted her. Cupping her breasts in his palms, he lifted them just above the water and licked the moisture off her nipples. First one then the other. Her moan vibrated along his skin like a caress, making his cock harder. "I want you. I want you now, Alastriona, right here." He lifted her up by her waist and as her legs snaked around him, he turned and laid her on the padded decking surrounding the tub. As he covered her body with his, he slid into her, rocked hard and deep.

"Bradley, I need to come, I want to come now. Please hurry." She tilted up and using her legs as leverage, surged against him, taking him deeper inside. Her moans became whimpers, then sobs.

He took her nipple into his mouth and suckled it hard, his tongue pressing the nubbin hard against the roof of his mouth. His cock was pulsing inside of her, her heat, her wetness driving him on to the ultimate goal.

"Come for me, baby. Come all over my cock. That's it, baby, tighten around me, pull me deeper. Come! Now!" Her explosion was epic; her scream rent through the morning quiet like a gun shot. Bradley felt the moment she started to come again, the moment her body pulled him along. He poured into her, deeper and harder than he'd ever come before in his life. He knew, knew with all certainty, that they had created a child, their child.

Chapter Forty-Eight

He carried her into the cabin and up to bed. Reverently, he put her to bed and covered her up. He laid down beside her and simply watched her sleep, marveling again and again that she was his and she was safe. Finally, he fell asleep, but not before joining her beneath the blankets and pulling her lax body close to his.

They were having breakfast that evening when Mel showed up. She said that she was there to answer any questions they might have.

"Did you know that Christopher was going to show up last night when you sent me to the field?"

Mel looked over at the beautiful woman, more so now that she and Bradley had become one. "Yes. And, before you ask, no, I couldn't have told you. Sometimes fate needs a helping hand, not a shove down the stairs. You needed to make the choice to go or not, and the decision to confront or not. Each generation has had the same opportunity to become the king and queen of wolves. No one made the decisions needed to make it fact." She stood to go to the sink, thought it was too much work, and sat back down. With a small wave of her hand, a cup of

235

steaming tea and a plate of her favorite cookies appeared on the table between them.

"Are you saying that everyone failed before now? No, I don't believe that. My dad and mom were good people, and never would have done anything different than we did." Bradley snatched a cookie off the plate, only to have one replace it immediately.

"Last night was your decisions, the two of you. Your parents had a different one. And no, it was never a question of failure, just as yours would not have been for you. It wasn't even the outcome, but the way you each depended on the other ultimately. As you said last night, beside you, not behind." When he looked at her sharply, she shrugged.

"Are you saying that he and I are now king and queen of wolves because we worked together? That doesn't make sense. I mean, all those before him could not have made it work as well as they had without working together. That isn't possible." Airic took a cookie off the plate and watched as another replaced it. She looked at Mel.

"The magic knows to trust you, so it shows itself. And no, what you did wasn't just working together, because you're right, they all worked as one. You two depended on each other, ultimately. You knew without doubt that Bradley would protect you, even if it meant his death. Just as you, Bradley, knew that she would do the same, even if it meant death. No doubts, no second guessing."

After a few minutes of quiet contemplation, and another cookie, they started talking again. Mel was relieved. And a little nervous. She knew this next part wasn't going to be easy.

"So now what? We're the king and queen, our marks are different. I don't see a crown, so that's not different. What are we now that marks us a royalty?" She watched as he sat back in his chair, then reached over, snatched Airic up, and settled her on his lap.

Just like the vamps, she thought, *always touching.* She smiled. *Yes, this was a good decision for everyone.*

"There is a crown if you want it, but it's hard to keep it on your head when you run as a wolf, I would imagine. You'll both live a lot longer, well, that's not quite true. You're now immortal like me. Your children will also be immortal, and you're right, Bradley, you created a child last night, a boy child. You now have magic, quite a bit as a matter of fact. I will send someone around when you're ready to be taught how to use it. As king and queen, I'll expect you to be with a bodyguard at all times. I know you're immortal, but you can still be hurt." She stopped and looked at them and realized that they hadn't heard anything she'd said past the child. Oh well, that was okay. They had lifetimes to learn their new duties.

She picked up her cup, put it in the sink, and the plate of cookies disappeared. She shimmered out of the room without either of them noticing.

About the Author

Hello! My name is Kathi Barton and I'm an author. I have been married to my very best friend Sonny for at times seems several lifetimes – in a good way, honey. And together we have three wonderful children and then the ones we brought into the world - Paul and Dale Barton, Jason and Wendy Barton and Danielle and Ben Conklin. They have given us seven of the greatest treasures on Earth. They don't live at home seven days a week! No, seriously, seven grandchildren – Gavin, Spring, Ben, Trinity, Sarah, Kelly and Kian.

www.ingramcontent.com/pod-product-compliance
Lightning Source LLC
Chambersburg PA
CBHW032211190626
46810CB00019B/2658